EDWIN P. HOYT served in the U.S. Army Air Corps and in the Office of War Information before he became a war correspondent for United Press International. He also worked for both the *Denver Post* and the American Broadcasting Company in the Far East, Europe, and the Middle East in the years following World War II. Hoyt is the author of many military history books, including *The Men of the Gambier Bay*, *McCampbell's Heroes*, and *Bowfin*, as well as the War in the Central Pacific series: *Storm Over the Gilberts*, *To the Marianas*, and *Closing the Circle*.

THE SEA WOLVES

GERMANY'S DREADED U-BOATS OF WW II

EDWIN P. HOYT

AVON
PUBLISHERS OF BARD, CAMELOT, DISCUS AND FLARE BOOKS

AVON BOOKS
A division of
The Hearst Corporation
105 Madison Avenue
New York, New York 10016

First Avon Printing: June 1987

AVON TRADEMARK REG. U.S. PAT. OFF. AND IN OTHER COUNTRIES, MARCA REGISTRADA, HECHO EN U.S.A.

Printed in the U.S.A.

K-R 10 9 8 7 6 5 4 3 2 1

CONTENTS

CHAPTER ONE

The Athenia *Sets the Course of War*

Late in August, 1939, the German naval high command prepared for war at sea, and obeying the orders of Admiral Karl Doenitz, all the operational U-Boats of the fleet were scattered about the water where potential enemies might be found. Of the 50-odd submarines available, 18 were sent to cross and cover the western approaches to the British Isles, through which ships coming from North and South America must approach Great Britain. And of the 18 U-Boats so positioned, fatefully, the *U-30*, under *Oberleutnant* Fritz-Julius Lemp, would find itself in position to strike the first German blow against enemy shipping—and in so doing would set in motion the chain of events that determined the course of the sea war.

Lemp was a round-faced, stocky young officer in his middle twenties trained aboard sailing ship and steam vessel in naval duties and then picked by the meticulous Admiral Doenitz as one of the elite, the corps of U-Boat commanders for whom Doenitz and all Germany had such high hopes.

His vessel was a Type VII Atlantic U-Boat, capable of travelling 6200 miles on the surface at 10 knots, able to make a maximum speed of 16 knots, quite fast enough to capture or overtake most merchantmen. She carried five torpedo tubes, a four-inch gun to fight with on the surface, and an anti-aircraft *Oerlikon*.

The U-Boats were spread out in grids that season, and Lemp's area was a blank space of blue on the charts, 36,000 square miles, extending from 54 to 57 degrees North Latitude, and from 12 to 19 degrees West Longitude, a vast panorama. Here, when the expected war came, he would be responsible to see that no military vessel passed safely and that all cargo vessels and passenger steamers were scrutinized and treated under the laws of the Anglo-German Naval Treaty of 1935 and the London Submarine Protocol of 1936. The latter agreement provided that submarines would behave very much like surface vessels in their approach to commercial shipping. A submarine commander would surface, stop a ship—perhaps by firing a shot across its bow—and examine it. If the ship was a neutral, carrying a cargo to a neutral port, it would be let go. If it was an enemy vessel, or a neutral carrying a cargo to any enemy port, it might be sunk or captured. In any case, the agreement called for the submarine to give full warning to allow the crew and passengers to get off safely in lifeboats. Even further, the submarine commander was responsible to see that the crew and passengers had a reasonable chance of making port safely, depending on conditions of wind, weather, and the proximity of rescuing vessels. If the crew could not be guaranteed safety otherwise, the submarine was supposed to take the crew aboard, its tight quarters notwithstanding. If the crew could not be taken aboard, the ship should not be sunk.

These rules were thoroughly understood by *Oberleutnant* Lemp when he sailed from the submarine base at Wilhelmshaven early on the morning of August 22 and headed into the North Sea. He travelled up close to the Arctic Circle, then turned west, and south through the mist and fog that lie in this area in the best of times, and found his voyage as peaceable and quiet as could be expected.

Oberleutnant Lemp patrolled his area then, or lurked there, as his enemies would put it, and he waited. Soon enough came the word from Doenitz' headquarters that negotiations with Poland had failed and that war against the neighboring state had begun. But that message did not materially affect Commander Lemp or the men of the *U-30,* for what they were waiting for was more serious.

As was expected in Berlin, British Ambassador Sir Nevile Henderson made demands on the German foreign office for removal of German troops from Poland, and when they were refused, war came. At 1:30 p.m. on September 3, 1939, Admiral Doenitz at his submarine force command post near Wilhelmshaven received the order from Berlin that war had come. Doenitz closeted himself with his maps then. Later in the afternoon he went to his post at the Neuende Naval Radio Station in Wilhelmshaven, which was to become a nerve center for the U-Boat fleet. There Doenitz conferred quietly with Admiral Boehm, commander in chief of the fleet, and Admiral Saalwechter, commander of Naval Group West. It was not a happy conference, for the other two admirals were gloomy about the prospects for victory, and even Doenitz was subdued by the realization that he would need 300 U-Boats to do what he wanted, and he had only 57 available. But his confidence did not evaporate. Indeed not. The trim, neat, and well-ordered Doenitz smiled thinly to show that confidence. Before him lay Directive Number One from the *Oberkommando der Wehrmacht* (OKW), the supreme war command of all Germany. The order had been issued four days earlier when the likelihood of war seemed immediate, and it called for the waging of *guerre de course,* or war of pursuit, against England. It was just what Doenitz wanted, although he had pleaded for many more U-Boats than he had, and he knew better than anyone else what the problems of the U-Boat war would be.

At the end of the meeting, at 5:15 p.m., Doenitz handed a message to an aide and ordered that it be put in code and sent to all the U-Boats then at sea.

"Commence hostilities against Great Britain immediately," said the message. "Do not wait for attack."

Those words reached *Oberleutnant* Lemp very shortly. Already that day he had heard of the British declaration of war against the Third Reich, and he was moving slowly through his operational area. But only when the order came from Doenitz did the U-Boat captain leave the control room of *U-30*. He headed then for the tiny, curtained compartment that served as his private quarters. He picked up the sealed envelope that held his orders and broke the seal hastily. And then he read his orders, which were much what he had expected. Then he went to the bridge of the surfaced U-Boat to begin his first war patrol. The great day had arrived at last!

Training was one thing; war was quite another, and the excitement and responsibility of leading a crew of nearly 50 men were heady spirits to a man of 26 years. Lemp knew his laws of war and he also knew that they were not uniformly liked by members of the German U-Boat service. There was question as to whether or not really effective undersea warfare could be conducted within the bounds of these old-fashioned and gentlemanly rules. *Oberleutnant* Lemp was also only too well aware of several hidden dangers he might face. In the last war, when Germany's submarines had begun to assume a definitive threat to British sea power, the enemy had pursued the U-Boats with fast, heavily armed merchant ships converted to "auxiliary cruisers." The British had also used Q-Ships, which were apparently merchantmen but which carried heavy guns and flyaway bulkheads and even depth charges to harry the U-Boats. All these matters were very much on the young submarine captain's mind that afternoon as he joined the watch on the bridge and trained his glasses around the horizon. Below, the torpedomen had already armed the warheads of their deadly weapons.

This afternoon of September 3, the weather had been changing. Before the sea had been calm and the wind just blowing enough for comfort, a delightful sea breeze. But by late afternoon, as the light began to fade a little, the wind kicked up to Force 4, which meant that the waves bore whitecaps and were deeper and rougher than they might have looked to a landsman. The wind drove the water against the U-Boat and made the scanning harder. The clear sky turned hazy, and the horizon lowered and shifted. The men braced themselves on deck to maintain even footing as the submarine headed north through the waves.

Just before five o'clock in the afternoon the sun set, and the shadows began to lower. Captain Lemp swept the sea with his glasses as before. Then he saw something, off to starboard, on the horizon. It was a ship, a very large ship, approaching off the bow. *Oberleutnant* Lemp called *Leutnant-zur See* Peter Hinsch to the bridge. Hinsch was the gunnery officer and would be in charge of the deck gun if they went into action on the surface. They hailed the approaching ship and prepared to stop her.

But should they stop her? Was it safe even to try? Before sailing *Oberleutnant* Lemp had been briefed by Admiral Doenitz on the vicissitudes of a U-Boat commander's life, and high among these was the danger of being entrapped by an auxiliary cruiser which would appear to be a prize ready for the picking but would then endanger the submarine. The more Lemp looked through his glasses into the haze in the shrinking light, the more he was convinced that before him moved an armed merchant cruiser. He had expected that the British would move quickly to protect their merchant shipping, and here seemed to be the proof of it. Under the circumstances it seemed foolhardy to continue to approach the other vessel on the surface. So thinking, Lemp acted, and in a moment the siren calling the men to battle stations surged through the U-Boat, dragging men out of their berths, and even from the most intimate chores of cleaning up in the heads. Lemp gave the order, and the U-Boat's tanks were blown, the vents opened, and the sea invited in. The ship began to dive, leaving a smaller and smaller wake as the superstructure disappeared, and finally even the telltale streak of the top of her disappeared.

U-30 began a careful approach to look over the oncoming ship. "Up periscope," shouted Captain Lemp, and the U-Boat's eye began to rise on its long stalk.

The captain bent down to the awkward position he must assume on these boats to look through the scope and stared intently into the eyepiece. With his cry for the alarm, and the diving, the ship had swiftly changed over from propulsion by her two diesels to battery operation, and now the submarine moved quietly through the water beneath the surface at periscope depth. Lemp turned until the U-Boat was travelling on a southwest course, which would bring him into position for a front attack, so he could send his torpedoes across the other's path.

What was she?

It was growing dark now on the surface, and it appeared even darker through the tiny lens of the periscope. The big ship was not showing lights, which a passenger or merchant vessel should certainly be doing, according to the rules. There was every chance she was a true enemy and not just an innocent barge. *Oberleutnant* Lemp was convinced of it. He decided to attack.

Tracking the surface ship through the lens of the periscope, he called for bearings, and an enlisted man gave them to him. In the control room the fire control mechanism began to work, and the wheels were in motion. He took one more look, and then began the firing run, raised the periscope again, not quite a mile away from the other ship.

Fire One. The first torpedo left the tube.

Fire Two. The second torpedo followed.

Fire Three. Out went the third.

Fire Four. Out—no, not out at all—was the fourth and last torpedo of the spread. It was stuck in the tube, a danger to every man aboard the U-Boat.

Suddenly the fate of the target ship seemed very unimportant; at least in Lemp's mind it was overshadowed by the need to get rid of the stuck torpedo. He dived, and like a big sea fish trying to throw a hook, the U-Boat struggled underwater for her own survival.

In the meantime, the ship on the surface headed confidently, unknowingly, directly into the path of *Oberleutnant* Lemp's torpedoes. The ship was

dark, and she intended to be dark, to attract as
little attention as possible on her voyage across
the Atlantic to the coast of North America. There
was nothing ominous in her darkness, she was
blacked out by Admiralty instructions, for her
own safety. She was what she seemed to be, in
spite of *Oberleutnant* Lemp's suspicions. She was
the Donaldson Atlantic Line ship SS *Athenia,*
heading for Quebec and Montreal. She was a
fine, if not entirely modern, vessel of 13,000 tons,
carrying 1100 passengers, most of whom were
women and children, many of them Americans
and Canadians bound home hurriedly from vaca-
tions and business trips, hastened by the threat
of war. The *Athenia* had sailed from the River
Clyde, and Glasgow, headed for Belfast and then
the West. She had stopped and anchored at the
mouth of Belfast Lough, taken on frantic passengers there, and stopped again at Liverpool on the
Mersey, where Captain James Cook had gone
ashore to consult with naval control officers. After some time ashore the captain had returned,
bearing new sailing instructions—he would not
follow the usual great circle route. Instead he
would steer a course 30 miles north of usual. He
was warned to take extra care and especially to
watch out for U-Boats.

Captain Cook had taken his warning seriously.
The crew checked the lifeboats, 26 of them; the
life rafts, 21 of them; and the 1600 life jackets.
All was well. The naval instructions told him to
prepare for war, and he did, not knowing if it
was coming. He was particularly concerned about
the dangerous waters they would traverse on the
western approaches, but he estimated that they
would be out of these waters by late afternoon
and relatively safe from U-Boat attack.

Captain Cook and the crew and passengers of
the *Athenia* learned of the war before noon, ear-

lier than did *Oberleutnant* Lemp and his crew. The captain had the boats checked once again and the plugs put in the lifeboats, where in peacetime they were kept out so rainwater would drain from the boats. The captain also kept very much to himself, concerned about the responsibility he bore for the passengers and afraid that he might somehow reveal his worry and frighten them into panic.

At six o'clock, the chief officer took the watch, and as dark fell checked the portholes and other openings to be sure the blackout shutters were operating. The captain appeared in the First-Class dining room at dinner, and all seemed to be well. Twilight began to lower. Then, from the lookout in the mast came a shout, and anyone who heeded and looked out to sea might spot the wake of a torpedo, a little stream of white pushing through the water, like a fish playing along the surface. But the fish moved meaningfully toward the ship, and then a torpedo struck, smashing the vessel's side near the Number 5 hold, killing some passengers and crew outright, injuring others, and throwing the well-ordered life of the ship into confusion.

Precisely what happened next was never determined. Passengers and crew said they saw the U-Boat on the surface, and some said she fired shells at them from her deck gun. The Germans, in their report, claimed never to have surfaced but to have spent the next period trying to shake out their faulty torpedo. Only one of the three torpedoes that actually fired went on to hit the *Athenia,* but that was quite enough. Within three minutes her officers knew she was sinking.

With a minimum of confusion, officers and men of the crew got the lifeboats out and began moving people into them. Half an hour later, *Oberleutnant* Lemp ordered the U-Boat to surface, and she came up in the darkness to see the *Athenia* listing badly and lifeboats in the water around her. Then came the shocker. The radio operator came up on deck and silently handed Lemp a piece of paper.

"*Athenia* torpedoes 56.42 north, 14.05 west."

It was a message sent out by the operators on the stricken liner, and it sent a wave of fear and worry through *Oberleutnant* Lemp. He had been specifically ordered to leave passenger liners alone, and here in the first hours of the war, he had violated the cardinal rule set down at the London Conference of 1936. He had torpedoed an ocean liner carrying men, women, and children, and particularly one that he knew must be carrying many neutrals. (There were more than 300 American citizens aboard.) One of the major reasons for German adherence to the Protocol of 1936 was the general staff's deep belief that America might not have entered the war of 1914–18 on the allied side had she not been driven to it by Germany's policy of unrestricted submarine warfare, which had resulted in such disasters as the sinking of the liner *Lusitania*. Grand Admiral Eric Raeder, commander in chief of the German navy, was known to hold these views, and it was understandable that a mere lieutenant would blanch when he contemplated what he had unwittingly done.

Lemp was so visibly shaken that even the stuck torpedo was forgotten for a moment while he asked why, why this had happened to him. Then he got hold of himself, concentrated on blowing the stuck torpedo from its tube, and moved quietly away from the scene, keeping radio silence and proceeding with his patrol.

Aboard the *Athenia* people were dying, and one of the first to go was a 10-year-old girl, killed by debris from the blast of the torpedo. Below decks cabins collapsed and people were thrown into the hold to drown or die of wounds. Some were catapulted down a deck or more, through debris and water. In the saloons dishes and glassware crashed and splintered. The hands rushed to the decks to man the lifeboats, and on the bridge the officer of the watch worked the mechanism that closed the watertight doors of the compartments. The boats began to go over the side, with a minimum of panic, and while some male passengers behaved badly, the crew controlled them. Within a very few minutes the distress signals began to go out, first in naval code and then in the clear, and it was these messages that *Oberleutnant* Lemp received to his shock. Other ships heard and responded. A Norwegian tanker started up from 40 miles to the southwest, not really believing the liner had been torpedoed. Captain Cook destroyed his code books and the ship's log, weighted them, and threw them overboard. The boats continued to leave the ship, filled with people in every state of dress and nakedness. There were accidents, one boat was dropped and several people were injured, but shortly after nine o'clock, the ship still floating, all but two of the boats were launched. Before 9:30 other ships had begun to answer the liner's distress calls, but they were still a long ways away. The *Athenia* would float for 15 hours before she would die, but no one knew that, and the evacuation was soon complete. In the lifeboats and in the water there were scenes of heroism, and also of injury and death, and in all 112 people would lose their lives in this tragedy, 95 of them women and children, and many of them neutrals.

By late evening the world was beginning to learn of the torpedoing of the ocean liner. London's newspapers had the story for their morning editions. In Washington, next day, President Roosevelt's press secretary considered the matter important enough to make a White House statement, pointing out that the ship was not carrying munitions or any war goods. The anger and worry of the uncommitted nations of the world began to mount, and in Britain, where suspicion of the Germans and their methods went back a long way, there was not much credence given the belief that the British ships *must* be armed and that the Nazis could be expected to break all the "civilized rules" of warfare.

In the morning, as the Admiralty tried to ascertain what had happened through ship-to-ship traffic, the torpedoing was definitely established, and so was the surfacing of the U-Boat, as far as the British were concerned. The 1300 survivors of the *Athenia* became heroes in the eyes of the world; the Germans became the beasts. Even in neutral Ireland, whose sympathies were seldom with the British, the tide of feeling against the torpedoing was high, and when some of the survivors were brought there by the Norwegian tanker *Knute Nelson,* nothing was too good for them; they were met at the docks and the people of Galway would accept no payment for any goods or services from them.

As for the Germans, it was an entirely different story. Germany, official and unofficial, was appalled at the charges made by the British—and for a very good reason. *Oberleutnant* Lemp had maintained total radio silence, not knowing how to handle what he knew to be a horrible mistake. Consequently, on September 4, when Admiral Doenitz and those much higher up learned of the charges being made against Germany by half the world, they were dumbfounded.

OKW—Supreme Headquarters—denied flatly that any German submarine had been within 75 miles of the sinking on September 3, and the German foreign office charged that the British were faking. They indicated that the British were so low that they would even sink one of their own ships, at great loss of life, and then put the blame on the innocent Nazis.

Adolf Hitler, the Fuhrer himself, came into the picture. He was intensely interested, because at that point in history he did not want to run any danger of forcing the United States into the European war on the side of Britain. He asked Doenitz for the story, and Doenitz came to headquarters to report. The U-Boat commander in chief assured the dictator that no U-Boat could have sunk the ship, and then Germany's leader made the fateful decision to pull out all the propaganda stops. Josef Goebbels' ministry of propaganda was given the order to deny everything—and as was the way in a police state, the Fuhrer's will then became "instant history." As far as facts were concerned, the issue was closed.

At U-Boat headquarters there were some queasy stomachs. Doenitz could see from his maps that if an over eager *Oberleutnant* Lemp had exceeded his orders and moved into his operational area before the time came to commence war—then *U-30* might have been responsible. This was what had happened.

> "*U-Boat Atrocity*"
> shouted the world press.
> "*British lies*"
> shouted the German propagandists.

And so the matter continued, with public opinion in the uncommitted nations becoming inflamed with every new survivor story, every tale of the unwarranted deaths of the 112 who had died of shock, of explosion, of crushing between boats, in the propellers of the rescue ships—and in other horrible ways, all detailed by newspapers for the people to read.

As the news and propaganda war raged, Admiral Doenitz was almost too busy to notice. On September 4 came the first British air attack on his submarine facilities. Bombers struck the Wilhelmshaven locks and the ships in the harbor, and while they did not meet any real success, Doenitz watched grimly from a submarine tender and predicted a long and bloody war for the navy.

Two days later, Doenitz' fears were realized, in part. *U-38* began stalking a British merchantman, with every intention of following the honored rules of war—and then the merchant ship fired on the U-Boat the moment the captain of the ship caught sight of the submarine. This was no way for a merchantman to act. Actually, the evidence of the *Athenia* had helped make the British leaders decide that they would arm their merchant ships and fight the U-Boats. The merchantmen also had orders to use their radios, and special signals———SSS———SSS———SSS——— which meant submarine, and thus call for help as soon as they were threatened. The simple fact was that knowing the potential, knowing the history of the past, the British simply did not trust in Nazi adherence to international agreement about submarines, and they were prepared to fight a total war against them.

Nor was it long before others accepted the British view. One day *U-3* reported from the North Sea that she had stopped the Swedish neutral ship *Gun* one night in bright moonlight. The captain of the neutral vessel came aboard, as was prescribed by international law, and brought his ship's papers with him. The U-Boat captain did not like what he saw in the papers: the Swedish captain claimed to have aboard 36 tons of explosives destined for the Belgian government, but the ship was not following a course that would take her to Belgium. The German captain decided to take the Swedish ship as a prize and ordered a prize crew from the submarine to board. The prize crew was rowing over to the *Gun* when someone aboard the Swedish vessel decided to take matters into his own hands. The Germans came aboard and began to take over the duties of the crew. Suddenly, the Swedish ship got underway and pointed her bows directly at the U-Boat, obviously intent on running down the submarine. The captain of the U-Boat shouted for full speed ahead on the diesels, and just barely managed to slide by in front of the speeding merchant ship that threatened her. The furious captain then sank the merchant ship.

But the Germans were still worried about international opinion, and Hitler had issued his orders. Doenitz transmitted them to the U-Boats at sea. "By order of the Fuhrer and until further orders no hostile action will be taken against passenger liners even when sailing under escort."

Aboard *U-30,* still at sea, *Oberleutnant* Lemp read that message and squirmed.

The experiences of the war were being added up both at the British Admiralty and at German naval headquarters. *U-48* stalked the British merchant ship *Royal Sceptre.* When the submarine surfaced and sent a shell across the ship, the merchantman began using her wireless. Out went the signal for all the world to hear: "shelled by submarine." And then the ship gave her position. The submarine commander was furious; he turned his guns on the ship, then put a torpedo into her and sank her. The captain said the merchant ship had violated international law by using her wireless.

Strike another blow against the gentlemanly conduct of war. Down went the *Royal Sceptre,* and in London the British naval authorities said again, under their breaths, "You can't do business with Hitler," and prepared for all-out war. It did not matter that *Korvettenkaptaen* Herbert Schultze stopped the British ship *Browning* and ordered her to help survivors of the *Royal Sceptre,* not to the British. The war increased in intensity. Guenther Prien, commander of *U-47,* came upon the British merchant ship *Rio Claro* one of those early September days. The weather was fine and fair, and the Prien surfaced. The merchantman stopped, but she began sending the hated SSS——SSS——SSS signal, even when a warning shot was sent across her bow. Prien ordered his gunner to put some shells onto the bridge. Three 3.5-inch shells screamed over and exploded, and the wireless fell silent. The boats came pulling away from the ship, but the captain had forgotten his papers. More delay, then the *Rio Claro* was sunk, which took even more time. Prien considered trying to find a neutral ship to pick up the survivors in their boats. But just as he was considering this course, he heard the sound of approaching planes—responding to the steamer's call for help. Prien dived, and the boats were left floating on the water, at sea, the survivors abandoned by their enemy. Another blow against the rules had been struck.

On this same patrol so early in the war, *Kapitaenleutnant* Prien took another lesson to heart. He approached the British ship *Gartavon.* The Britisher saw the submarine, began to use her wireless, and turned to make a run away from the enemy U-Boat. Prien's gunners fired the deck gun, and a lucky shot knocked out the aerial. So much for the wireless. A boat pulled away from the *Gartavon,* and he relaxed; then the steamer suddenly speeded up and headed straight for the U-Boat. Prien's orders came thick and fast. The U-Boat began to move, ever so slowly it seemed. The deck gun began to spit, and shells slammed into the side of the steamer. On came the British ship. The U-Boat was making way now. Prien could read the lettering on the bow: GARTAVON—it loomed larger and larger. And then, just as it seemed inevitable that they would crash, the U-Boat skidded by, missed so close that the bow wave of the steamer caught the stern of the submarine and slewed it halfway around. Prien regained control and caught his breath, then chased down the lifeboat. Her captain was in it, and so was the crew. They had rigged the helm speed at the U-Boat and then escaped the ship. Now the *Gartavon* was moving in a crazy circle. Prien was furious, but inwardly he admired the tough English captain. He refused to wireless for help, and the Englishman did not seem to expect anything at all.

So came the sinking of the *Gartavon,* and another tale that divided hunter and hunted even more firmly than before.

As the warm September days sped by, the U-Boats moved into port and the commanders appeared to make their reports in person to Admiral Doenitz, who asked them pointed questions and began to draw conclusions. The captains reported, and their stories grew redundant: wireless ... blackout ... attempted ramming ... approaching aircraft ... forced to dive.

Admiral Doenitz communicated his views to Grand Admiral Raeder, and that admiral spoke to Hitler. On September 23, the Fuhrer changed the rules for the submarines to conform with the practice already adopted by the U-Boat captains. All merchant ships in the future which used their wireless on being stopped by U-Boats would be sunk or taken. So the merchant captains were given a Hobson's choice: keep quiet and run the danger of being abandoned at sea without anyone knowing what had happened to them, or shout out the warning SUBMARINE and be sure to lose their ship. Almost uniformly the merchantmen chose to take their chances with the wireless rather than the mercies of the U-Boat commanders.

Four days later, *Oberleutnant* Lemp brought *U-30* into port at Wilhelmshaven. Admiral Doenitz stood at the lock gates as the U-Boat moved slowly into the base, and he did not seem to see the birds flying in the harbor that day, or hear the music of the band that had come down to serenade the conquering heroes.

Lemp came ashore to report, visibly upset. He asked almost immediately to speak to his commander in private, and when they were closeted, he confessed that he had sunk the *Athenia* thinking she was an armed merchant cruiser.

With an effort, Doenitz controlled himself, although he did tell Lemp he would have to court martial him for disobedience of instructions. The unhappy Lemp nodded. He knew. But it was more serious than that—so serious that Lemp was dispatched that very day by air to Berlin to report personally to the naval high command. He was taken to see Admiral Raeder himself.

Raeder heard and was disturbed. The German press and radio were trumpeting the official line laid down by Goebbels: there had been no sinking except perhaps by the British themselves for propaganda purposes. No U-Boat had sunk the *Athenia!* Hearing, knowing, Admiral Raeder took his alarming news to Hitler and Hitler made the fateful decision that almost from the beginning destroyed the credibility and even the tradition of the German navy. Hitler ordered that the sinking of the *Athenia* be kept a secret.

It was simple enough to deal with Lemp. His career, even his life, depended on his superiors and their good will. The unhappy U-Boat captain went back to Wilhelmshaven, where Doenitz interrogated him at length, and then placed him under cabin arrest. Lemp was still threatened with court martial.

But there could be no court martial in view of Hitler's orders. More, Lemp's silence was not enough, because in the normal course of events eight copies of the log of a returning U-Boat were made for official and training purposes. Now history must be rewritten. The pages of the log that referred to the *Athenia* were excised in the original, and the log was faked at U-Boat headquarters. Goebbels' propaganda machine never stopped its lies about the *Athenia*: she was carrying munitions (untrue) she was carrying gold (untrue) she was sunk by Churchill's own orders (untrue and outrageous.)

Who then in England would now believe that U-Boat war could be anything but frightful?

German submarine commanders had not all made Lemp's mistake. When Schultze sank the SS *Firby,* he sent a message by radio to Winston Churchill himself, telling him to pick up the crew and where to do so. It was a joke, and bravado, but also informative. Schultze had endangered his U-Boat by this act of humanitarianism. But by this time even in September, the British looked upon the act and saw the bravado, not the bravery. Another U-Boat commander, Heinrich Liebe, put his men to rescuing survivors from a tanker's oil fires, even though the tanker had used her radio when he struck. He gave his crew's life jackets to the enemy survivors and called for a neutral ship to rescue them.

Another submarine commander treated some of the wounded who had been hurt in action against his boat. Another righted a number of capsized lifeboats and made sure the crew of the vessel he was sinking were safe and sound before leaving them. U-Boat commanders gave positions and even charts to survivor crews in their lifeboats, and sometimes provided them with food and water. But the war was taking such a turn by September's end that none of these things made any difference, and the pressure was on both sides for quite a different war.

CHAPTER TWO

The Ace of Aces

Doenitz needed a victory. It was the first of October, 1939, and the U-Boat war was not going anywhere nearly as well as the Germans might hope and the enemy might fear. The rules of warfare covering the merchant ships were being changed in fact by the actions of Germans and British, and the movement was steadily toward unrestricted U-Boat warfare. But on October 1, a doleful Doenitz wrote in the U-Boat Command's war diary that the salient matter of the moment was the shortage of U-Boats at his disposal. The success of his plans to build up the U-Boat arm depended on securing the backing of no lesser figure than Hitler himself. To gain Hitler's backing Doenitz needed a spectacular victory, and that meant in the military line.

The military record so far was spotty. On September 14, west of the Hebrides, *Kapitaenleutnant* Gerhard Glattes had spotted the British aircraft carrier *Ark Royal* at sea. This carrier and the carrier *Courageous* had been detailed to the western approaches to help fight U-Boats. Before the month would end, the Germans would sink 39 ships, with a gross weight of 150,000 tons, and the British were trying to stop them. When Glattes

saw *Ark Royal* and began to attack, the carrier
was unaware of his approach and submerged; he
was able to send three torpedoes at her. But the
Germans were having torpedo trouble just then,
the triggering device on the torpedoes failed this
day, the magnetic detonators simply did not work,
and all three torpedoes exploded prematurely.
Ark Royal was unhurt. She was warned, however, and her destroyer screen was turned loose
to find and sink the submarine. Three destroyers
surged down on the *U-39* as she tried to escape
and staged repeated depth charge attacks. Glattes
was unable to go deep enough, unable to twist
and turn and escape, and eventually he was forced
to order the ballast blown and the submarine
surfaced. She came up literally in the midst of
her enemies, and there was nothing to be done
but surrender. The men abandoned ship. The
submarine sank, and Glattes' crew became the
first submariner prisoners of the British in World
War II.

The score was evened a few days later. *Korvettenkapitaen* Otto Schuhart in *U-29* was waiting
on the approach from the west to the English
Channel. It should be very good hunting here in
this part of his patrol area, and it was this day.
The submarine was at periscope depth on the
morning of September 17, waiting. The men were
having their morning coffee, in fact, when the
turning periscope revealed a 10,000-ton steamer
approaching from the west, flying a red flag. The
ship looked very suspicious indeed because she
was moving fast, and she was zigzagging, as
though she had something to fear from a U-Boat
and also something to hide. But several ensigns
of the world were marked in red, and Captain
Schuhart strained at the periscope, trying to make
out the nationality of the steamer.

He spun the scope. His plans changed hurriedly, his decision made, when he saw a blob near the ship's stern. The blob moved, *flew* over the ship's stern—it was an airplane, and it must be an English airplane, and thus this must be a ship of the English and furthermore a valuable ship. It must be carrying something very important, and that meant guns or supplies for the military or troops. Thus reasoning, Captain Schuhart decided to torpedo the ship and ordered his torpedo room to stand by, ready for orders that would send the explosive missiles on their way.

Just then, the target zigged and turned away, showing her beam to the submarine. She was too far for a shot. He would have to wait for her to go over the horizon, then run ahead to intercept her and cut across her course. All this meant surfacing and then a chase. It would take time, and there was no hurry. Schuhart ordered the boat to drop down to 120 feet and relaxed. He ate a sandwich and drank a cup of coffee.

When he estimated that enough time had lapsed, Schuhart headed for the surface, but being a prudent captain, he stopped at periscope depth and took a look around. Off to port he saw a cloud of smoke. He watched it, and the cloud became an aircraft carrier, heading toward him. Before the lowered periscope he also saw the mast of one of the carrier's destroyer escorts. He looked around the circle for aircraft. There was none. He moved ahead then, toward the enemy, and informed the crew that they were after a carrier.

U-29 stalked. Schuhart kept his eye to the periscope and watched as a destroyer appeared in front of the carrier, and then another on each side, and then one astern. He saw a plane, and then another one, and they seemed to be circling and watching. He was very careful, moving alongside his quarry as he zigged and zagged. Then, although he did not like the position, he saw that the carrier was making a sharp turn away from him and might escape altogether. He was facing into the eastern morning sun, another strain, but still it seemed to be now or never. He gave the order, the tension was too great after two hours of stalking. Fire!

Three torpedoes sped away from the tubes of the U-Boat, and immediately, guessing that whether they hit or not they would attract the attention of the guardian destroyers, Schuhart headed for deeper water. The port destroyer was only 500 yards ahead of him. Down went the U-Boat—80 feet, 100 feet, 120 feet, 140, 160—they passed the safe limit of 150 which had been ordered as maximum depth in peacetime—and still Schuhart took her down. They hit 180 feet, and he listened for the sounds of strain on the hull. She seemed safe enough. He also listened and heard another noise—a popping, an explosion, and then another one just like it. Two hits on the carrier! And then came lesser explosions. Something was happening inside the enemy ship. She was breaking up, the torpedoes had spawned little explosions of their own.

The British were coming now, and the men in the U-Boat could hear the buzzing of the approaching propellers. Then they were the hunted, and the new hunters were right over them. The propellers began to die out; the enemy was moving away. But then, one after another, came four tremendous explosions which struck the boat and pushed her down and from side to side. The submarine actually trembled.

This first pattern of depth charges was followed by another, and by another. The U-Boat lay deep, quiet, and waited, every man's heart pounding.

Above, the destroyers faced a terrible choice. The carrier—for it was HMS *Courageous*—was mortally wounded and listing heavily to port. Fifteen minutes after the torpedoes struck, she shifted, capsized to port, floated keel up for a moment, and then sank to the bottom. Into the oil that covered the water went 682 men, but 518 went down below, including the captain of the ship. And when the waters closed over the carrier, the destroyers had those oil-soaked men to consider. The Dutch liner *Veendam* was close by, and she came to help with the rescue, but the destroyers had their work cut out for them. After the three depth charge attacks, they moved away from the submarine, and some went to the rescue. Schuhart and his men continued to hear depth charges, moving farther and farther away from them, until nearly midnight, when they felt safe enough to surface. The U-Boat was saved to fight another day, and all that could be seen was flotsam and the dark stain of oil on the water.

This had been a success. Much as it hurt, the British announced the loss of the carrier next day, and in a strange way the laconic announcement took much of the steam out of the German boasting. Doenitz needed more success than this, and many more U-Boats. He had expected to have nine new boats by October 1, but only three of them were ready. He was using the little, old *canoes*, as they called them, the 250-ton coastal submarines of a much earlier design than the Atlantic U-Boats that he wanted. The canoes were valuable but troublesome because they were too small and not powerful enough to meet Doenitz' demands. One of them, however, had already given Doenitz the spark of an idea for a grand military coup, an attack against the British fleet anchorage at Scapa Flow, far to the north.

Doenitz dreamed of attacking Scapa Flow. During World War I two brave U-Boat commanders had made the attempt, but the British fleet was wary and they had both failed, although they had gone down as heroes in the annals of the German submarine force. Doenitz, of course, had cubbed in that force and the names of *Kapitaenleutnant* Ensnann and *Korvettenkapitaen* von Hennig were seared on his memory. Even before the war was declared, Doenitz was thinking of the merry hell his U-Boats could play among the battleships and cruisers of the Home Fleet once they got in among them in these Scottish waters.

When war broke out, Doenitz had first of all asked OKW in Berlin for a complete report on Scapa Flow. In September he had acquired new aerial photographs which showed the disposition of the British ships. And then, one day in September, *Korvettenkapitaen* Wellner, commander of the little canoe *U-16*, had come home from an operation in the Orkney Islands area with a detailed report on the perimeter defenses and conditions of the area. Wellner had been working around Pentland Firth, the passage that ran between the Scottish mainland and the Orkneys, and had been caught in a strong current while submerged. The electrical engines of the little canoe were not a match for the current, and try as he might, Wellner could not escape its pull. So, since he was in no danger from enemy attack, he realized that he had an opportunity to observe conditions in this vital and mysterious area, and he relaxed and watched and made notes as he drifted along. He remained in the vicinity of this enemy stronghold for many hours, and timed the patrols and observed the lighting conditions and the strength of currents. Then he went home and reported in detail to a fascinated Doenitz. If a large and powerful submarine could do as he did, and waited until the submarine nets and booms were open to let in ships or patrol vessels, and followed one through, then Wellner was certain that a successful attack could be made. Getting out—that was something else again, and he did not give it much consideration, nor did Doenitz. The attack was the thing.

Doenitz' aerial photographs showed the whole area, and he began studying them again. Yes, Wellner had something. Given a little luck and a brave and determined captain, a U-Boat might make it into the enemy anchorage and play havoc. It was certainly worth a try. Doenitz ordered up more photographs from naval headquarters. He looked at all the entrances. Hoxa Sound, Swith Sound, and Clesstrom Sound all led into the fleet anchorage, and all were well guarded. Holm Sound was completely blocked by two merchant ships which seemed to have been sunk diagonally across the Channel, and then there was a third ship north of them. But there was another narrow channel about 50 feet wide, a little over 20 feet deep to the south in Holm Sound. Also there was an even smaller channel close to the shore on the north. A good navigator, a careful captain with plenty of courage, might just make it in and out.

The choice of captain was everything. But here the U-Boat commander was on very familiar ground, for he *knew* his men, their capabilities and their potentials. His U-Boat captains were not chosen at random; they were the pick of the sea service. From among them available at the moment, he chose Guenther Prien, the captain of *U-47*. Prien was a slender, thin-faced man, a martinet who drove his crew unmercifully, but a cool-headed submariner who could be counted on to risk everything if need be. He called in Prien. He also called in Wellner.

Kapitaenleutnant Prien had just come back from

leave after his first war patrol, pleased to discover that *U-47* had been refurbished and was very nearly ready for sea. There had been a little work into the dockyard, the stores were aboard, the fuel had been replenished, and the crew had come back from leave before him and was undergoing training exercises.

Waiting for assignment could be fretful business, but not this time. Just back, on Sunday morning, this first Sunday in October, Prien was called to Doenitz' office, which in this case was aboard the tender *Weichsel*. He went, and there in the wardroom he found the flotilla commander and *Korvettenkapitaen* Wellner.

The other two went in first, while Prien fretted in the wardroom. Then it was his turn, and he entered the admiral's office, where Doenitz, with the aid of the other two, laid out the prospect of attacking Scapa Flow. Charts and photographs littered the table. Wellner had his story ready. Doenitz outlined the opportunity and then began to sketch the difficulties: the 10-knot current in Pentland Firth, the guard boats, the patrols. But there were pluses: the shores next to those narrow channels were completely uninhabited. At slack water between tides, at night, a U-Boat could get through.

Doenitz talked. It was to be a voluntary mission, he said. He did not want an answer at that moment. He wanted Prien to take the materials with him, study the file for 48 hours, and then come back with an answer. No matter what he decided, Doenitz promised, the answer would not affect the Prien career in the slightest. It might really not be feasible to make the actual attempt, no matter how good the plan looked on paper.

Secretly, of course, Doenitz was convinced that it could work. His operations officer, *Korvetten-*

kapitaen Oehrn, thought so too, and Doenitz trusted Oehrn's judgment more than that of any man on the staff. So the pressure was very much on Guenther Prien.

Prien was equal to it. He was a determined and ambitious young man who had come up through the merchant service, gaining his master's papers at the age of 24. He started all over as an ordinary seaman in the navy in 1933, worked his way up to become an officer, and a U-Boat officer at that. He had served during the Spanish Civil War with *Leutnant* Werner Hartmann in the *U-26* when Hitler sent submarines to aid the Falange's cause. He had gone to submarine commander's school and had gotten his own U-Boat, the *U-47*. And he had distinguished himself on his first war patrol. He now took the materials from the file and went over them carefully. Obviously, Admiral Doenitz had already decided that the project was possible. Doenitz was not in the habit of propounding theoretical questions to his U-Boat captains. So he must show his enthusiasm and his grasp of the project. Prien studied for a day, then wrote a report which he revised to give more strength, and well within the 48-hour period he appeared again at Doenitz' door; the messenger escorted him into the office, and he waited to report.

Doenitz kept him standing before the desk, waiting, then asked the question. What about it? Prien said he was ready. They shook hands, and the U-Boat captain went out to make his final preparations.

Prien sailed then, on the morning of October 8, with orders to carry out his penetration of the British anchorage on the night of October 13. The crew and his officers knew nothing of the plans; they were secret to begin with and Prien was never one to fraternize or become chatty with his subordinates. So officers and men of the *U-47* moved out in mystery as they sailed through the Kiel Canal and into the North Sea. For all they knew they were going on a normal patrol to sink what they might find in enemy waters or on the high seas.

The first indication that something strange was afoot had been the removal of some stores from the U-Boat. Prien's decision to lighten the boat was inexplicable, but submarines are used to accepting the inexplicable as normal. A man who could trust his life to an "iron coffin" was beyond worry about any little thing just out of the ordinary. Second, when they achieved the North Sea and were moving along through satisfactorily dirty weather which obviated any troubles with the British blockade of Germany, Prien ignored the merchant shipping around him. The watch on the bridge saw smoke clouds, Prien saw them, and said nothing at all. And so they moved north, toward the Orkney Islands. The weather continued dirty, with dark nights and heavy seas that splashed foam across the U-Boat like snow. Finally, early on the morning of October 13, they came in sight of the Orkneys in the light of the night sky. Prien looked around him, satisfied, and then gave the order to dive. He told the boat chief to take her down to the bottom.

Once on the bottom, the boat secure, Captain Prien called all hands forward into the torpedo room. They crowded in like fish in a school, sitting on the bunks, leaning against the bulkheads, and the executive officer quieted them and reported to Prien that they were ready. Then the captain of the submarine came forward to speak.

He told them where they were going, into the British lion's den. It was an assignment suitable to impress every man on the boat, and the men listened carefully as the captain told them to get all the rest they could because they must be at their best during the coming few hours. The men off watch were told to turn in and sleep.

The U-Boat lay quiet on the bottom until four o'clock in the afternoon. Prien moved into his stateroom—curtained off from the rest of the boat—and lay down to rest. At four o'clock in the afternoon the men arose and the cook served a hot meal. The men were almost gay; their morale could not have been better, for they had high regard for this slender, taciturn captain of theirs. They ate carefully and the messmen began to clean up after them.

At 1915 it was time to begin moving. Prien had checked his charts; he knew them by heart, and so now did his officers. The ship was called quietly to battle stations, the main vents were closed, the ballast was blown, the motors started, and the U-Boat moved toward the surface. Prien stood in the conning tower, bent down, and ordered the periscope raised. He peered through the eyepiece into darkness, and then the scope broke water. Quickly he spidered around, scanning the circle about the boat. Nothing. It was safe to surface.

The U-Boat splashed up through the water, a low gray silhouette resting confidently against the sea. The water had quieted in the evening from the blow of afternoon and morning; the sky was still overcast. Good enough. But there was something else, something not good at all. The northern horizon was ablaze with the *aurora borealis,* and at times the whole sea seemed to be lit up, like the *Friedrichstrasse* on Saturday night. If that was an exaggeration, the excess of it did not affect the U-Boat men. Their lives were at stake, and they were hoping for every slender advantage the god of submarines might grant them. The lights flashed and Captain Prien frowned. But there was nothing to be done. They must move on.

The U-Boat moved into Holm Sound, its diesels churning with a noise that suddenly seemed very loud. Even the wake seemed noisy tonight. Prien was tense on the bridge. Suddenly his eye caught a shadow. What was it? A ship? Quietly he gave the order to dive, and the U-Boat went down to periscope depth. Prien raised the scope and peered—indeed, it was a ship, and he was fortunate to have been so alert.

They moved along, toward their objective, back on the surface. Prien was not pleased. The wind was blowing away his clouds, and the visibility was growing by the moment. Those damned northern lights threatened the whole mission, casting shadows from anything that rose above the day.

At the edge of Holm Sound, the channels narrowed around two tiny islands that blocked the waterway above Burray Island and protected Scapa Flow's entrance. Here in the narrows, just as Wellner had warned, the current was swift and fierce, pulling them inward now, toward the place they wanted to go, but almost controlling the U-Boat's passage, and that would never do. Prien was choosing the northern-most narrow channel so he might conceal the U-Boat beneath the overhang of the shore. The current caught them, the struggle was terrific as the U-Boat men used all their skill to keep the bow of the ship steady. One danger followed another—the worst of them those moments when they seemed to be bearing down steadily on one of the block-ships. If they collided, no matter how easily the U-Boat got off, the resulting racket would endanger their mission. They might all end up the war in a British prison camp.

But Prien saw the danger in time, and they moved below the blockship. Down past Glimp's

Holm they went past the headland hanging down from the north, and then they were in Scapa Flow. They had done the impossible: they had penetrated the inner reaches of the British fleet anchorage.

Still on the surface, Prien looked around. To the south there was nothing. He looked north and saw the shadows of ships, so he turned the U-Boat that way. Travelling quietly along the coast to the north, soon he saw two battleships, and beyond them several smaller ships at anchor also, which he presumed to be destroyers. As the U-Boat moved up he could make out details and identified one of the battleships as *Royal Oak* class. (She was indeed *Royal Oak* herself.) He identified a second ship as *Repulse,* but here he was wrong. (She was *Pegasus,* a superannuated seaplane carrier.)

The submarine was below the surface now that they approached so close, and Prien invited his executive to share the look through the periscope. He began to give orders.

Ready the tubes.

The tubes were clear.

Ready tubes one, two, three, four.

The tubes were ready.

The executive officer was to do the shooting. He took aim on the *Pegasus.* He pressed the key, and the torpedoes fired.

Then came the anxious moments. They crawled by. Whoosh? There was action: a tall column of water shot up against the side of the seaplane carrier, or it seemed to be the seaplane carrier. Actually, the first torpedo had hit *Royal Oak.*

Prien was on the alert, ready for anything. Would the alarms sound, would the searchlights go on, would the battle begin and the probing fingers of the destroyers come out to feel through the water for *U-47?* Not at all. Prien looked through the periscope and looked again. The anchorage was much as it had been. There seemed no especial activity aboard either big ship. What had happened?

Actually, when the first torpedo struck *Royal Oak,* the explosion, forward, seemed to the officers to have been something internal, and while they were concerned, they did not consider it to be a matter of life and death. They had not the slightest suspicion that offshore there was lurking a German submarine.

It was shortly after one o'clock in the morning. The silence was incredible to Prien, but it was his mark as an able U-Boat commander that he chose to capitalize on it. Obviously the British had no idea he was there. They were not launching a counterattack. He could fight some more this night.

Prien ordered the ship to the surface and swung around through the bay. There was absolutely no sign that his presence was noted. He gave the orders to reload the tubes and headed back, on the surface this time, for a second attack. If the British cared so little, he would attack above water. And this time, his contempt was aroused and he came in even closer than he had approached submerged and fired a salvo of torpedoes at the overlapping ships. The confidence was endemic; one of his junior officers went out on deck, away from the safety of the conning tower hatch, and Prien had to call him back.

This time, the pyrotechnics were more pleasing. One explosion followed the other. Columns of water snarled up, followed by gouts of smoke. A whole gun turret blew up, and tons of armor and debris flew into the air. Now, this time, the harbor came to life. Internal explosions nothing—the British realized that something was afoot. Lights began to come on. Ashore, vehicles started up and raced along the roads. The British were coming to life.

It was time for *U-47* to get out of Scapa Flow—if she could manage it. The dreaded searchlights of the destroyers were snapping on now and flashing across the water, searching, searching. A light—the headlights of a car—turned out to sea and toward the U-Boat. Was the driver just turning around, or had *U-47* been spotted?

On the surface, Prien moved the U-Boat swiftly back where he had come, now to find that he faced a strong surging current that moved against him. Just then, behind, a destroyer seemed to be moving toward him. Prien shouted to those below to give him every ounce of power, fighting the current, to move out through the dangerous narrows, to get to a point where he could dive deep and fight off the depth charging if it came to that. The diesels turned and groaned, but they gave their power, and the U-Boat inched through the current. Behind, only too visible to the captain of the submarine, the destroyer was moving, and her searchlight was prying across the water. She was signalling someone, too. Would she head toward them and find them?

The struggle with the current continued. But now, the destroyer turned back, moved away— and then suddenly the U-Boat surged through the narrows, so close inshore that Prien could see a wooden pier dangerously near as they moved by. And as that shock sank in, he heard and felt the rumble of depth charges. The British were bombing something inside the harbor, but whatever it was, it was not *U-47*. They were through and clear, miracle though it seemed to be.

Prien headed south now, back, toward Wilhelmshaven and his home base. The crew was jubilant and wanted to commemorate the great day. Someone had an idea: during the hours of waiting the men had laughed over a cartoon book which featured a bull with its head down and nostrils breathing smoke. How appropriate. They approached the executive officer, and as the submarine sped along the surface of the North Sea in the daylight hours a working party went on deck and painted a snorting bull on the side of the conning tower. The Bull of Scapa Flow—that was to be the crew's nickname for the ship.

On the way home, the men of *U-47* discovered that they had made Guenther Prien famous. German radio announced the British reports that *Royal Oak* had been sunk in Scapa Flow, apparently by submarine attack. And later, the official German radio announced that Prien was the man who had done the job.

As the U-Boat moved south, events stirred within Germany. Scapa Flow had a special meaning to the German people, for it was here that the German High Seas Fleet had been ordered at the end of World War I, and here that the officers and men of the German navy had scuttled their own ships rather than turn them over to the hated British. So Prien had passed over hallowed ground, the bottom of the harbor littered with the wreckage of German history, and in the sinking of the mighty battleship he had avenged the disgrace of the German people. Of that second salvo, two torpedoes had hit *Royal Oak,* and she had rolled over in 13 minutes and capsized, killing 24 officers and 809 men, even as Prien was racing off through Kirk Sound, passing the southern blockship and Lamb Holm. What matter if *Royal Oak* was too old and too slow to be a ship of the modern British navy's line. The propaganda value was immense: all the world was impressed with the daring of the German U-Boat men.

In Berlin, Admiral Raeder was jubilant, Adolf

Hitler even more so, and he ordered that Prien be given a hero's welcome. So when the U-Boat made its way into the Wilhelmshaven harbor, she was escorted by two destroyers, and there was Admiral Doenitz, waiting. More, beside him on the jetty stood Grand Admiral Erich Raeder, come to do honor to the man who had salvaged a shield of German honor. When the boat was stopped, Raeder came aboard, shook hands with every man of the crew, and conferred on every one the Iron Cross, Second Class, which was a medal granted few enlisted men by a navy that reserves its awards for officers. Prien was given the Iron Cross First Class for leading the exploit. And more, he was to have the honor of reporting directly to Adolf Hitler on the accomplishment.

That day the Fuhrer's personal airplane came to Wilhelmshaven and picked up the whole crew, to take the heroes to Berlin. There was a parade from the Tempelohf airfield to the Kaiserhof hotel—a grand establishment reserved for admirals and other superior beings at most times. Crowds surrounded the heroes and pressed their hands and made it almost impossible for them to move. Then, finally, they were taken to the Reich Chancellery to meet Hitler himself. The dictator shook hands with them, spoke to them, and then conferred the Knight's Cross of the Iron Cross on Prien—making him one of Germany's first prime heroes of this war. Prien had a private audience with the dictator then, while the crew waited, and then they all went to lunch as Hitler's guests. In the afternoon, they fell into the hands of Dr. Josef Gobbels' propaganda ministry and held a press conference. Then, for the next few days captain and crew were lionized by Berlin and all of Germany and given special leave.

Meanwhile, Admiral Doenitz, who had accomplished just what he expected with the Prien

exploit, was moving feverishly to capitalize on
the victory. As he knew, the British became
alarmed when they learned that a submarine
had penetrated their main fleet harbor and decided to move the fleet until they could make
Scapa Flow safe from undersea attack. He anticipated that the British would move their big ships
into Loch Ewe, the Firth of Forth, and the Firth
of Clyde while they sealed off the ratholes into
Scapa Flow. He decided to divert some of his
submarines from the job of sinking merchant
ships and harry the British fleet. Meanwhile, he
also put the political wheels in motion to secure
the permissions he needed from Hitler to widen
the range of submarine warfare. Soon Hitler
agreed that enemy ships could be torpedoed without warning and that passenger ships in convoys
could be destroyed. Then *all* German restrictions
were removed from enemy passenger ships, and
the area around the British Isles was declared
hunting ground for anything at all. Month by
month the wraps were taken off, until finally
there would be no more at all.

Doenitz' plans were very well conceived indeed. Even before he had sent Prien to run the
gauntlet at Scapa Flow, the submarine commander had dispatched another very competent
U-Boat captain to the western entrance to the
Pentland Firth, which was an approach to the
Orkneys and the fleet anchorage. This was Otto
Kretschmer, the cigar-smoking young commander
of *U-23*, for whom Doenitz had hopes as high as
those for any submariner. Kretschmer was not
quite 30 years old, son of a teacher from Lower
Silesia, and a sailor who would rather be at sea
than anywhere else in the world. Where Prien
was bright and quick of wit, biting in sarcasm
and old-fashioned German martinet toward his
men, Kretschmer was more broadly humorous,

more human. Yet he also was noted for a contempt for weakness, intolerance, harshness toward any who failed their duty. Already, as war broke out, Prien and Kretschmer were beginning a competition as hunters of the sea. Prien had been tapped for the first big assignment. Kretschmer had gone out in September to lay mines in the Scottish coastal waters to be troubled by torpedo failure which prevented his sinking any ships. On October 1, he sailed again, for Pentland Firth. On the three-day trip to the Orkneys, he sank a small coastal steamer, the *Glen Farg,* then Prien got the nod and sailed, and Kretschmer's patrol area was changed, away from the Orkneys.

Doenitz sent *Korvettenkapitaen* Habekost out in *U-31* to lay mines off Loch Ewe, figuring that some British capital ships would come into that area. One did, the battleship *Nelson,* and she struck one of the mines and was damaged. *U-21* went to the Firth of Forth and laid mines. Not long afterward the new cruiser *Belfast* struck one of them and broke her back. And the damage alone was not a true indication of the trouble Doenitz was just then causing the British fleet. *Belfast,* for example, could not even be sent back to the big naval dockyard at Portsmouth for repairs until the mines had been swept up, and it took the British weeks to clear the area so they could risk sending the crippled cruiser for repair.

Prien went out again in the middle of November to the area around the Shetlands, but he found no traffic there and headed for the Atlantic. He was singularly unlucky for so ambitious a man, and except for one neutral, passed no ships for days. He tried to attack a destroyer, but she began a run down on him and he dived deep to escape. He came across the cruiser *Norfolk* and torpedoed her—or tried to—but his torpedo exploded in the cruiser's wake. He did not know that and reported cockily that he had just sunk an eight-inch gun cruiser. (He had dived after firing and heard the explosion, came up and saw nothing, so assumed he had been victorious.) The German radio made the claim then, because anything Prien did was food for the Nazi propaganda mills now. But it was not true. A few days later Prien encountered a convoy of nine steamers escorted by a handful of destroyers. He managed to sink one 10,000-ton passenger steamer, but depth charging then drove him to the bottom to stay until the convoy had passed beyond the horizon. Then, on this same patrol, he found a tanker and blasted her in half. Another tanker, this one 9000 tons. But that was all. He ran out of torpedoes and headed home. This patrol had in no way matched the last one.

Meanwhile, another young U-Boat captain was doing much better. He was Joachim Schepke, a tall, very charming officer who had come into the U-Boat corps at the same time as Prien and Kretschmer. He shared the same driving ambition and egotism, and he was out sailing this autumn against merchant shipping, in *U-19*, one of the little "canoes." In two brief days of patrol, in the tiny boat that carried only five torpedoes, he sank four ships which totalled 20,000 tons. By the end of the year, all the U-Boats together had sunk about 500,000 tons of enemy ships, which represented 114 merchantmen. Other names were becoming famous too, that of Herbert Schultze of *U-48*, who would be the first captain to sink more than 100,000 tons of ships. Then there was Werner Hartmann in *U-37*, who led the first coordinated effort of the U-Boats against a British convoy on October 17, 1939. He took two other submarines against a convoy off Cape Trafalgar, near the northwest shore of the Strait of Gibraltar, and in a few short hours they sank three of the ships, although the convoy had air cover.

The war was entering a new phase.

CHAPTER THREE

The Atlantic War

It took the Germans a little while to get going. From the beginning of the war, Admiral Doenitz had conceived of the "wolf-pack" idea as the proper method of employing his U-Boats. But he did not have the boat power to do it at the beginning, and although Hartmann in *U-37* had some success, it was marred by torpedo failure and the small number of wolves in the pack. There just were not enough U-Boats available yet to carry out the kind of war Doenitz wanted. So he sent the boats out singly for the time being to see what they could accomplish. The sea-going or Atlantic class boats were sent into deep water, while the little canoes with their short range were kept close to the continent and their bases.

Kretschmer in *U-23* went out again in February and was very nearly ambushed by a British submarine. Luckily he saw the telltale tracks of torpedoes and dived away in time. Otherwise Hitler would have then just lost one of his most impressive U-Boat commanders. This was the trip on which Kretschmer got a destroyer. It was the middle of the month, the U-Boat had been out for a week without seeing any action, and this evening the captain went up on deck to look over the horizon and smoke one of his big black cigars. He was fuming away when out of the murk came a destroyer, escorting a convoy, less than a mile from the submarine off the starboard bow. Kretschmer decided to attack, and more, to attack on the surface.

So the captain pointed the bow of the little submarine at the destroyer and fired two torpedoes, swung the boat around and began to move as fast as the diesels would carry her. *U-23* had scarcely made her new course when behind them came a roar, that meant explosion, and then the destroyer rolled over and sank.

Kretschmer had seen another destroyer on the other side of what was obviously a convoy. One might have expected him to run hard now because of what he had done—for there is no enemy like a wounded enemy, and the sinking of the warship must have aroused all the others. But run? Not at all. Kretschmer turned back and steered parallel to the convoy, trying to catch up with her again. While doing this he began to have some luck: he ran into a lone merchant ship which was steaming along in the dark. He attacked again, with no torpedoes, and sank the freighter, which was the *Tiberton*.

One torpedo left. That was all on this little canoe. It was three nights later that the chance came to use it, while Kretschmer was cruising near the Orkneys. He came then upon the freighter *Loch Maddy,* about 5000 tons, and with his one fish he managed to sink her. Then it was time to go home. Kretschmer had one more patrol in the little *U-23*, but then his exploits were such and his success with Doenitz was so great that he was given a new command. He had made nine patrols in the little canoe, sunk eight merchantmen and a destroyer, laid mines, gathered intelligence for Doenitz, and exceeded his instructions with his diligence.

The new submarine, which he was to commission, carried a crew of 44, and, which was more important, 12 torpedoes, and could stay comfortably at sea for six weeks at a time. Further, she could cruise far out into the Atlantic and catch the ships bound for Britain outside the protective cover of the air umbrella that the Royal Air Force could throw up.

Thus, at just about the time Kretschmer's *U-99* was ready for sea, in the summer of 1940, began what the U-Boat men called "the happy time," when they roamed the Atlantic and sank British shipping almost at will it seemed. Doenitz had been hard at work for months, among other things solving the torpedo problem. It was going to take some time to really solve it, but for the moment, the magnetic explosive device was abandoned and contact firing pins were used. By June, 1940, most of the U-Boats had been in the dockyard, and refitted, and Doenitz was very hopeful that he could really carry the war to the enemy. Kretschmer went out, up through the North Sea, heading for the passage between the Orkney Islands and the Shetlands, and then into the Northern Atlantic, and then approaching the sea lanes that brought ships to Britain from the west. At first he operated as a loner—that was the way it was set up by Doenitz. On July 5 he sank the 2000-ton ship *Magog,* and then gave a bottle of brandy to the captain to ease the pain of being in the lifeboat.

He sank the Swedish ship *Bissen,* and the liner *Humber Arm,* and after the second attack he was viciously depth charged, although he took the boat down to 350 feet. This *was* an experience. Kretschmer and the crew sat below the surface while the enemy ranged back and forth above, listening for any sound from the submarine. The U-Boat shut down every motor that could be stopped, but some electric power had to be maintained to keep the boat under control and deep enough. The British came and came back again, for two hours, dropping depth charges that fell very near the U-Boat's hull. At the end of the two hours, one charge came particularly close, shaking the whole boat. And then the oxygen supply failed, and the men had to put on the special rubber breathing masks the U-Boat carried.

On went the battle—for it was a battle just as surely as if Kretschmer had been above the surface. The corvette above ran in and ran out again, banging away with those lethal charges of explosive in their odd barrel-shaped cans.

The third hour went by. The attack continued. The fourth hour passed. The tension was eased for a while when the cook served out emergency rations of chocolate. The fifth hour passed, and the Britisher did not give up. Then came the sixth hour, and there was a lull. Had he gone away? Kretschmer did not know. He waited.

The answer came in 45 minutes. The attacker had not gone away—he returned with another depth charging.

Matters were growing desperate. The U-Boat's air was foul, with the smells of humans and the stink of oil. But still they stayed below, suffering, and waiting, perhaps to die. They waited 12 hours and the boat was filled with its stinks and something worse—carbon dioxide, the breath of death.

There were many dangers. It was obvious that the British ship or ships above could sense their quarry. They had been travelling all this time, slowly, but the enemy had travelled right with them. It was the famous British Asdic, underwater sounding device, with which the destroyers

and corvettes were equipped, and with it the ship
or ships above could keep on top of the submarine. So far Kretschmer had been lucky, no depth
charge had come close enough. But wasn't it just
a matter of time?

And how much time was left? The submarine
was full of filthy air. Worse, it had been driven
down to 700 feet—about 150 feet below the absolute safe depth for this type of boat. Could they
go any deeper? Or would the plates begin to
buckle inward from the pressure, squashing the
men like so many pieces of raw red meat?

There was very little that Kretschmer could
do, but he could do something. He could at least
change direction. He ordered a turn to starboard,
hoping to throw the enemy off the beat. Perhaps
it was this change, coming at a time when the
enemy ship was distant, between runs. Perhaps
they had put a layer of current or cold water
between them and the British attacker. Layers
of water moved back and forth in the ocean, and
they had different sound characteristics, which
the U-Boat men would learn to use like airplane
pilots used cloud cover.

Kretschmer listened. More explosions—but they
were farther away. And ten minutes or so later
the next group came, still farther away. He kept
the boat moving, hoping. They moved for another two hours, until there was not enough power
left in the batteries to do more than start them
for the surface, and then they still stayed down.
They were supposed to run out, but they continued to give power. The Germans stayed down for
nearly 20 hours before they felt safe enough to
come up, and when the boat emerged on the
surface then, not a man had the strength immediately to stand and open the hatch. Finally
Kretschmer did, but it was 30 minutes before he

and the crew could do much more than lie on deck and gasp for fresh air.

But a few hours later, it was back to the business of killing. The ship sank the *Petsamo*, a 5000-tonner, then captured the Esthonian *Merisaar* and sent her home as a prize. They sank the steamer *Budoxia* and the *Woodbury*. That ended the dozen torpedoes, and Kretschmer signalled to base that it was time to come home.

Home had changed. With the fall of France to the German army, it was possible for the U-Boat to use French bases, which meant they no longer had to fight their way up north, around the top of the British Isles to get to the Atlantic Ocean, but could sail directly out from a French base, intercepting traffic on the way to Gibraltar, and making a straight shot to the western approaches where they could harry shipping coming to beleaguered England. Kretschmer and *U-99* were send to Lorient in France, and this was to become the home of the U-Boats, which would be protected from enemy air attack by huge "pens" built under thick concrete, blockhouses so complete that 1000-pound bombs had no effect on them.

From here, Doenitz proposed to inaugurate his new phase in the attacks on England. *U-37* had returned from her foray as leader of a wolf pack and in 26 days at sea she had sunk 43,000 tons of ships. Doenitz was really pleased and very nearly ready to begin the wolf-pack war.

Kretschmer and Prien and Schepke were all based at Lorient now and were competing with something a little less than friendly rivalry for tonnage. Indeed, their tonnage figures tended to be exaggerated. But they were good enough. On return from his patrol that took him into Lorient Kretschmer remained in port for a short time, but by July 24, 1940, was back at sea. And this time he was practicing a new technique—attack at night on the surface. He began with the sinking of the *Auckland Star,* using that method. There was one disadvantage: the ship fired back at him and forced him to submerge lest he be hit. He put a second torpedo into her from below. And then a third, before the ship capsized. A few hours later he sank the *Clan Menzies*—which cost him two torpedoes, and he finally also decided to send a boat with a sinking crew of demolition experts, before his ship nosed under. But then things picked up. He sank *Jamaica Progress* with a single torpedo. He came across another convoy, and sank *Jersey City,* with one torpedo. Of course there were attacks on him. At one point he was nearly sunk again by a British submarine but managed to avoid two torpedoes from the Englishman. He was harried and forced to dive many times by Sunderlands and other British patrol craft. But the planes, while they bombed and strafed and reported, had not yet achieved means that would come later in the war and really make life hell for the U-Boat commanders. Even the Admiralty at this point recognized the fact that the basic use of the planes was to keep the submarines down, which decreased their operating range and effectiveness.

Kretschmer was working on his sinking techniques this trip and making some innovations that were not in the book. This was all right—anything was all right with Doenitz, if it produced results. But if it did not, the U-Boat force commander had a steely eye and a sharp sense of discipline. A man could be out of the service for being out of line.

Kretschmer now broke a cardinal Doenitz rule: which was to fire a spread of torpedoes at the earliest possible moment. But the commander of *U-99* hated to waste torpedoes, particularly at long range. He now had a plan that he would try. It involved spotting a convoy in daylight, tracking it until dark (instead of closing and shooting while submerged) and then streaming in among the convoy ships in the darkness on the surface and attacking. One ship—one torpedo: that was Kretschmer's ideal. And so now he put the technique into motion. He would risk all on its success—and in this case all meant his life, the lives of his crew, and the U-Boat.

The convoy was the one he had spotted first on July 31, and from which he had already taken *Jersey City.* He tracked her, figured her course and speed, found her again, and followed. He then speeded up on the surface, passed the convoy (which was zigzagging) and got ahead of her. He waited until dark. This convoy was bound outward from the islands to pick up supplies. Kretschmer had a hunch that the escorts would leave the convoy at about a longitude of 20 degrees west, and he found he was right—they did leave that night, turned, and went to pick up an inward-bound convoy. And so, shortly after midnight, Kretschmer, like a fox in a henhouse, found himself in the middle of 20 merchant ships without any escort. He could not only attack on the surface, he could take the time and convenience to pick his victims. He chose tankers, which were highest on Doenitz' list. And so, spotting one in the second column, Kretschmer moved *U-99* right into the middle of the convoy on the surface, moved to within 600 yards of the tanker *Baron Recht,* and fired at point-blank range. The torpedo hit her near the stern and she began to sink. He turned to another ship, and fired once more. The *Lucerna,* another tanker, began to go down.

His next torpedo was a complete dud, which slipped over the side and headed for the bottom!

Now he was down to his last torpedo, which he had hoped to save for another tanker—but a freighter was in the way. Contenting himself with second best, he fired; just then the freighter turned, and the torpedo slid by her and smashed into the tanker, the *Alexia*. How was that for luck? Kretschmer was very pleased; he had sunk three tankers with four torpedoes, proved his point about surface attacks within the convoy, and made himself a legend in German sea lore. He returned from the patrol, flying the seven pennants that meant seven ships sunk, and now his U-Boat wore its own insignia too—a golden horseshoe, which was to become as famous as Prien's bull.

The toll of British ships was rising in that summer of 1940, and at home in Germany the propagandists were making much of the heroic captains who came home with their victory pennants high. The western end of the English Channel was still the best hunting ground, for here the U-Boats could go after ships destined for America or the Mediterranean and reroute them to the bottom of the sea. But behind all this was the directing genius of Admiral Karl Doenitz, for he was very much in command of the U-Boat force. When the U-Boats moved west to the French bases, he moved his headquarters to Paris for better communication with his charges. And while his men went out to patrol, they kept in very close contact with home base by radio, and through their reports Doenitz kept a running picture of the war at sea. He was so close to the action that if any two days went by without his having reports of ships sighted by U-Boats, he ordered the boats to new positions. It was a game of hide and seek, and Doenitz was constantly on the go.

That summer Guenther Prien distinguished himself once again, even as Kretschmer was returning from his experimental patrol. Prien was out in June, to the west of Scotland in *U-47,* and just as the patrol began he was finding life very dull—no ships to sink. After several days of inactivity he did find one target, chased it, and then abandoned the chase when he came upon a whole convoy, a huge convoy, the largest he had ever seen—42 ships sailing in seven columns. They were, to be sure, escorted by five destroyers, and that was a deterrent. But not a stopper. Prien began to track the convoy, but because of the escorts he tracked it underwater, and this was a disadvantage, because the Atlantic U-Boats could only make eight knots underwater. The convoy was faster. He lost it and had to content himself with a straggler, the *Balmoral Wood.* He sank her.

Two days went by, and it was June 16. Nothing. More time passed, then on June 21 he encountered another convoy of 20 ships and sank two more tankers, and then another, a Dutchman, and then another tanker. But look what he had missed. This did not please Doenitz at all. What was needed was coordination of these attacks, and so next time Prien went out that summer it was under different circumstances. Doenitz was perfecting what he called the *Rudeltaktik*—which means the flock or herd tactic in German. In English there was a much more descriptive and properly frightening term: the wolf pack.

This "happy time" of the Germans in the summer of 1940 was a reflection of Britain's organizational problems. There were not enough ships and planes to escort the convoys out into mid-Atlantic. From England the destroyers and planes took them out a few hundred miles. From Canada (for the U.S. was not yet in the war) destroyers and planes picked them up 400 miles off the coast. But there were many, many hundreds of miles at sea when the convoys were in danger. And it was here that the U-Boats could strike. Yet to what avail was it to have one U-Boat, even a Prien or a Kretschmer in command, in among a 30- or 40-ship convoy? The solution was to have a pack of submarines on call, which might attack all at once.

To do this, Doenitz must take tactical command of each operation himself. And that is what he planned. There was a big chart on the wall of the operations room of U-Boat headquarters, and Doenitz moved his pins around that board. The German cryptographers had done a good job of breaking the British codes, and often they could follow the course of convoys, but many times the signals came in or were deciphered too late for effective action.

Yet one day in September it all came together for Doenitz. He walked into the operations room and learned that the cryptographic section had picked up a signal four days before a homeward-bound convoy from America was due to meet its escort in the mid-Atlantic. There, before him, was the time and the place. He had the U-Boats at sea, and everything was ready. Not that things were not going well enough. In August the U-Boats, acting from their new bases, had sunk 267,000 tons of British ships—more than half as much as in all of 1939's war months. But it could be better. Doenitz was now about to show the world how.

Kretschmer in *U-99* and Prien in *U-47* were out. So were a number of other boats. Doenitz directed them to 19 degrees 15 minutes west, and there, in what the British called U-Boat alley, the Germans did find the convoy at the proper time. The weather was foul, nearly a gale blowing the seas so high that the U-Boats were smashed and battered as they plowed through the great waves in search of quarry. But the U-Boats got in among the "sheep" and on September 10 they sank five ships.

Kretschmer was having a run of bad luck just then: he had missed with three torpedoes. Prien had run out of them in this last attack and he wanted to go back to Lorient to reload, but Doenitz now showed what his form of teamwork meant. Prien in *U-47* was given the job of staying out on station about 750 miles west of the coast of England to deliver weather reports twice a day. Doenitz and his wolf packs were just beginning.

Prien sat on station and fumed. What was a prime commander of the U-Boat force doing out in the middle of the ocean without any weapons, giving *weather reports* like a lightship? He was furious, but he did not dare contravene the orders of his superior. Doenitz ran the U-Boat force, although his heroes might wax and wane.

But the famous Prien luck held. On September 20 a convoy from North America ran straight into his position. Excitedly he reported to Doenitz and got permission to become the "shadow" of the convoy, while the U-Boat commander moved swiftly to bring all the boats in the area up against the ships. Prien, like a gray shape in the night, trailed along behind or beside or even in front of the convoy, signalling its position, speed, and course. Back at headquarters, Doenitz went to the mapboard, moved the little symbols on a straight line up and down the path of the convoy, and sent the boats to those points. The U-Boats ranged across a front of 30 miles, on the surface, keeping in sight of one another.

Then Prien signalled again, and the U-Boats set out to intercept, travelling at high speed on the surface.

Kretschmer's *U-99* was one of the first boats to come up, and in the coming, he caught Prien on the surface, came so close that he frightened the watch of *U-47* (who were not doing their job), and then ticked off a furious Prien. (The competition among the heroes was growing fierce.)

Then there was work to be done. Kretschmer used his new technique. He watched the stern escort of the convoy until the destroyer zigged out on a wide leg and spread in toward the ships; then he was in among them. First came a tanker of 9000 tons, the *Invershannon*. One torpedo—smashing noises and flashes at the bow of the ship—and in moments the crew was taking to the boats. He turned, and then turned again as the destroyer outboard began shooting up star shells to illuminate the sea. He moved around to the dark side of the convoy and torpedoed the freighter *Elmbank*. She was a timber ship and devilish hard to sink. He put a dozen shells into her at the waterline, but all that happened was that the shells opened holes and the timber cargo spilled out. More shells. The ship stubbornly rode on. He sent another torpedo, but it struck a timber floatsam in the water and exploded before it hit the ship. He fired the deck gun again, and again—88 rounds of ammunition and still she did not sink.

Looking back, he saw that the tanker *Invershannon* had not sunk either, so Kretschmer took *U-99* back and put another torpedo in her. Then she broke in half, very satisfyingly, and went to the bottom. Back at the *Elmbank*, *U-99* was joined by *U-47*, which still had deck gun ammunition. Together they spent nearly all their shells on the freighter, but it would not sink until Kretschmer used phosphorus shells which set the deck cargo afire.

Kretschmer regarded the night as only partly successful and that was true from his point of view. But from Doenitz' station the story was all positive. Convoy HX 72 had come up to this point safely, 15 ships now travelling under escort. When the night was over, 11 of the 15 ships were sunk and one was damaged. And this meant thousands of tons of guns and planes and aviation gasoline that would never reach England. The wolf-pack technique had been proved beyond any argument.

As for the U-Boat commanders, their score was shooting up, and in Germany they were becoming even more heroic figures as the propaganda ministry boasted of their exploits. This was indeed "the happy time," and it reached a peak on the night of October 18, when six U-Boats combined to give the British a further taste of terror.

On the night of October 16, *Korvettenkapitaen* Bleichrodt in *U-48* was operating west of Rockall Bank, which was right on the British east-west convoy line, when he encountered an east-bound convoy of 17 ships, convoy SC 7, bound from Nova Scotia to England. As ordered, Bleichrodt reported immediately to Doenitz at headquarters, and the admiral began moving his little symbols around the plotting chart again. Within range were Kretschmer's *U-99,* Schepke's *U-100,* and three other U-Boats, captained by Frauenheim, Moehle, and Endrass—all names that were rapidly becoming famous in Germany.

U-48 shadowed the convoy that night but came too close and was driven beneath the surface by British depth charging. She lost contact with the convoy—and now Doenitz had to figure out how to regain it for his boats. He put a line of them across the possible routes once again and rushed out orders to the U-Boats, telling them the position they should assume by the morning of October 18, without fail.

In the morning the U-Boats were in place, at eight o'clock. But in London at this same time, the British Admiralty learned that *U-48* had been shadowing the convoy, and ordered drastic changes in SC 7's pattern. Then the British waited in London and Admiral Doenitz waited in Paris.

Frauenheim in *U-101* was the first to make contact with the convoy, and Kretschmer's *U-99* was only five miles away from him when they came upon the ships as dawn was breaking in the eastern sky. It would not be easy, the Germans saw, for now daylight was coming on and they could see the escorts, half a dozen including a number of modern destroyers.

And so they waited. All day long the wolf pack lurked along the fringes of SC 7, the British suspecting their presence, but unable to come to grips with so elusive an enemy. The U-Boats purred along, just out of sight or underwater, as the day wore on. Then came dusk, and the light grew dim. It was time.

Kretschmer in *U-99* moved in to attack and was training his sights on a ship on the outside when it disintegrated in front of him. An ammunition ship—torpedoed by one of his friends. The long night had begun.

The destroyers worked the fringes, driving the U-Boats down and away as well as they could. Kretschmer, for example, was forced to run away in the opposite direction by a speeding destroyer, and Moehle in *U-123* had to dive and stay deep, both losing contact for hours. But two hours before midnight Kretschmer was back on the fringe of SC 7, and this time shielded by the blackness of night. The other U-Boats fought in the traditional fashion, staying outside the screen, firing torpedoes. Not Kretschmer—he moved confidently in toward the starboard side of the convoy, between two destroyers, as fast as he could go. There were tense moments as he passed, but then he was through and approaching the outer column of the convoy, only 700 yards away.

Off went the first torpedo, speeding through the black water. It missed. Kretschmer could have kicked himself. It was bright night and the moon hung behind the convoy, silhouetting the ships for him, but he had missed. He fired again, and this time he did not miss. The ship broke up and sank with wretched crackling noises filling the air. She was down in 20 seconds!

Now ships were going down on the other side as the torpedoes of *U-46* and *U-100* and the others took effect. Kretschmer headed directly into the convoy, fired another torpedo, missed, and suddenly realized that he had a defective torpedo director aboard. He would fire at point-blank range, or by guess.

There was danger in the convoy. It came to Kretschmer suddenly, as a big cargo ship saw his submarine and tried to ram. She fired star shells as she came, and they broke above the U-Boat, sending flickering shadows down the line for all the convoy to see. Kretschmer dodged. The ship changed course and came on, determined. *U-99* retreated back toward the end of the convoy until the ship no longer endangered her, then turned and fired a torpedo. The "fish" ran straight, but the ship at which it was aimed then zigged, and the torpedo ran by. Yet there was a hit, for the torpedo struck another ship in another column, and it broke in two, then sank in about 60 seconds.

U-99 might have escaped then, in the confusion, but Kretschmer was not thinking about escape. He went back into the convoy, and this time he torpedoed another freighter. It must have been an ammunition ship, for it went up in a column of red-and-yellow flame and smoke that rose 500 feet in the darkness against the moon.

The escorts were busy now, charging back and

forth on all sides of the convoy. But they were not looking inside, where *U-99* was working. From 500 yards Kretschmer fired at one ship—she capsized immediately and sank—and then another—she broke in two. The other submarines were being forced down and were under attack. They could hear the depth charges but still Kretschmer went after the convoy. He came in to a range of 300 yards from a big freighter and torpedoed her. The distress signal went out from this one, *Shetaticka* was her name, and then they blew the bow off the freighter *Sedgepool,* which continued to drive ahead, shoved by the engines that pushed her beneath the sea. It was an eerie sight to watch the great ship go down, diving like a submarine.

The air was now filled with star shells. The escorts surged back and forth attacking, searching. But they did not sink a single submarine that night, hard as they tried. And when morning came and *U-99, U-101,* and *U-123* headed home, their torpedoes all expended, the wolf pack could count up 17 ships sunk for the night's work. That was 325,000 tons of shipping, the worst night's losses of the war for the British, and before the convoy got home it had lost 20 of its 34 ships. Small wonder that the British called the night of October 18 the Night of the Long Knives.

Kretschmer went home to receive his hero's welcome from Doenitz. Newspapermen and photographers clustered around as the men told the story of the attack and were lionized. And now Prien, off Rockall Bank, found another convoy and this time he had torpedoes in his *U-47.* Doenitz moved his ships on his private board once again, and a new wolf pack moved to the kill. Five U-Boats converged on this new convoy, HX 79. There were 49 ships, guarded by seven escort vessels, but the Germans got in among them once again, and when the night of October 19 was over and day appeared, HX 79 had lost a dozen ships. Prien, now extremely conscious of his tonnage figures, signalled back to Admiral Doenitz that he had sunk 50,500 tons himself. He went back to Lorient then and found himself the most celebrated U-Boat captain of all once again. He was the first to sink 200,000 tons of enemy shipping, and the total won him a new decoration: oak leaves in lieu of a new Knight's Cross of the Iron Cross.

Doenitz welcomed the decorations and the lionization of his men by Berlin, for it made his task easier and caused Hitler to listen to his pleas for more and better U-Boats. Remarkably, up to this point all that he had accomplished had been done by a handful of men. From May to October, the U-Boats sank 287 ships, losing six U-Boats in the process. The war had begun at a time when Doenitz had 57 U-Boats, and a year later he still had 57 U-Boats, 39 of them ready for operations. At any given time only a dozen were at sea, and he figured that with the time spent coming and going that at any particular moment there were only six U-Boats operating against the British.

So the dreaded wolf packs were no more than a single pack of hungry gray sea wolves.

CHAPTER FOUR

The Tide Turns

When Admiral Karl Doenitz saw how effective his wolf-pack technique could be in fighting the war of the Atlantic Ocean, he moved his headquarters from Paris to Kernevel, near Lorient, so he might be closer to his U-Boat men. Now he was even closer to operations than before; nearly every U-Boat commander saw him when he returned from patrol, and in the conferences of the Doenitz staff new ideas and new techniques came up every day. Doenitz did not miss many tricks.

The success of the submarines brought him what he wanted most: an increase in the submarine building program. But it was a dream, because in fact the program was reduced. In the second half of 1940 he got six new U-Boats a month. In the first half of 1941 he was supposed to get 29 boats a month, but actually got 13 a month until June, when the success of the past brought him 20 a month for a time.

November, 1940, seemed to pick up where October had left off; however, there was one difference. The weather in the Atlantic that year was especially filthy, and many U-Boat operations had to be called off because of it. At the beginning of the month there were no U-Boats at sea, but then Kretschmer went out again, and on November 3, he encountered three British ships: the merchant ship *Casanare* and two converted liners which had become auxiliary cruisers, the 18,000-ton *Laurentic* and the 11,000-ton *Patroclus*. First, he sank the *Casinare*. Then at 2200 he saw the *Patroclus* and the *Laurentic* and gave chase. Fifty minutes later he put a torpedo into *Laurentic* from 1500 yards. The crew began to go off in lifeboats. Half an hour later she still had not sunk. *U-99* fired again, but missed, and the steamer began firing star shells which drove Kretschmer away from her. He approached *Patroclus,* which was in the near area, and stalked her as *Patroclus* stopped to pick up survivors from the other ships. Just after midnight he was in position and fired a torpedo at the liner. It hit just forward of the bridge and 20 minutes later when the ship had not sunk, Kretschmer fired another torpedo, which hit aft. A third torpedo fired from only 950 yards hit below the bridge, but still the ship did not sink, so Kretschmer moved in, coolly to finish it off with gunfire. He hit her repeatedly, but *Patroclus* returned the fire.

Here Kretschmer was, steaming around on the surface, amid lifeboats and three stricken ships, all of which were sending their position to shore, and he was as cool as though he had been sheltered in one of the steel and concrete pens at Lorient base. Finally, about 2:30 in the morning (0230) a Sunderland flying boat came over, and he diverted, but only until the boat left, and then he surfaced to finish off the ships. He sank *Laurentic* with one more torpedo. He sent a fifth torpedo into *Patroclus* and sank her too. By now it was nearly six o'clock in the morning, and only now did a patrol boat or corvette come into the area and begin stalking the submarine. Kretschmer withdrew now, and at 1100 he dived because aircraft began appearing. But all this while, from 2200 for nearly 12 hours, the U-Boat had been able to do just as she pleased and sink three big British ships. It was a measure of the weakness and frustration of the British defenses at that moment.

But those defenses were improving very rapidly. The British had Asdic, the sounding apparatus that helped their escort vessels find the submarines. By January, 1941, they also began installing radar in their escort vessels. More of these were coming off the ways by 1941, which meant more surveillance of the waters around the convoys. And the British had perfected an anti-submarine device about which the Germans were slow to learn, a device that capitalized on the very procedure that Doenitz used to direct his wolf packs—radio.

To maintain tactical command of the wolf packs, Doenitz required that they report continually, so he could fix their positions. A U-Boat on weather detail was supposed to report twice a day. The British maintained a number of powerful radio reception stations in various locations, on the edges and in the Atlantic. Thus, whenever a U-Boat transmitted a message it was possible for the stations to pick it up, and through their direction finders to make a "fix" by triangulating the points and directions from which the transmission had been made. Prien, in particular, somehow sensed this, and he was the most unwilling of the U-Boat commanders to use his radio. In fact, Doenitz was often put out with Prien, as at the beginning of the chase of the convoy in September, when Prien's "shadow" reports were so few and fragmentary that Doenitz thought his commander had lost the convoy.

This strengthening of British defenses, plus the increase in number of aircraft, many of them coming from the still-neutral United States, brought about a gradual change in the war of the submarines and the convoys. It was best illustrated by certain events in the early months of 1941.

In February, Joachim Schepke in *U-100* sailed from Germany for a new patrol, Otto Kretschmer in *U-99* and Guenther Prien in *U-47* sailed from their base in Lorient, and all three of Germany's most famous submarine Aces were at sea. *U-47* sank several ships by the first week in March. Prien chased one convoy off the English coast but was driven down by patrol aircraft and lost touch. He found it again, sank a ship, and then was driven under by patrol craft which depth charged his U-Boat. On March 6, Doenitz had a new message from Prien: he had found another convoy. He was instructed to shadow it, and Doenitz sent all the other U-Boats in the area to form a wolf pack and attack. On the morning of March 7, Prien reported to headquarters again, giving the position, course, and speed of the convoy, and Doenitz sent this information to all the boats in the area, urging them on to the attack. *U-70* was one of the boats, Kretschmer's *U-99* was another, and the big boat *U-A* was still another.

On the night of March 7 the wolf pack struck this convoy, which was OB 293. In a short time two ships were sunk and two others were hit, but now the British escorts moved.

Lt. Comdr. J.M. Rowland in the destroyer *Wolverine* was one of these escort commanders. Just after midnight, Prien in *U-47* was moving along beside the convoy, on the surface, having attacked. *Wolverine* caught sight of his exhaust from the diesel engines, and the Asdic hydrophones were turned on. They verified the engine noises, so the destroyer speeded to 18 knots and began to chase the submarine.

Three minutes later Lt. Comdr. Rowland saw a wake on the surface of the water and speeded up to 22 knots, then caught sight of *U-47,* which was zigzagging rapidly across the water. Rowland was tempted to shoot, but withheld fire, hoping to close on the U-Boat further before Prien dived. It was no use, he was frustrated a moment later when the destroyer *Verity* fired a star shell, illuminating the area and showing Prien how close the *Wolverine* was coming. Prien shouted orders, and *U-47* dived.

The destroyer passed over the spot, and the Asdic operators strained their ears, but they could not hear the submarine below. Rowland turned 180 degrees and came back over the spot, the Asdic working—there he had a contact five degrees off the port bow. He moved across and dropped a 10-charge pattern of depth charges, set to run deep and explode. No results.

Nearly a quarter of an hour went by, the submarine hiding below, barely moving, and the men keeping quiet to try to outwit the enemy on the surface. *Wolverine* made contact again, ran across the spot, and dropped an eight-charge pattern. No results.

One might expect that the destroyer would give up, but not this one. Lt. Comdr. Rowland was a determined man. He continued to move and to listen. He enlisted the aid of the other destroyer, but the weather turned misty and they could not keep contact, even by talk-between-ships radio. So *Wolverine* continued the hunt alone. The Asdic was successful, and the submarine was relocated just before four o'clock in the morning.

Below, Prien was trying every ruse he knew. He understood that the British had some kind of underwater ranging apparatus, and he moved to throw it off the track. He dropped oil, which made a patch that the destroyer saw. He fired a torpedo out into the sea to lure the destroyer's attention away from his own course. But Lt. Comdr. Rowland was an old hand, too experienced to be taken in by tricks. Doggedly, the destroyer tracked the submarine, dropping depth charges, and hurt *U-47* so that she began to leave a telltale track of oil.

Prien very nearly escaped around four o'clock in the morning. He made it to a point nearly five miles from the destroyer, but the Asdic was so effective that even at this distance Rowland and his men could "hear" the submarine. Prien came to the surface and began taking evasive action, speeding this way, then changing course and speeding another way. But the destroyer speeded and slowed, the Asdic operator strained at his phones, and Rowland maintained contact with *U-47*.

Just after 0515 *Wolverine* spotted the wake of *U-47* once again through the mist, and a few minutes later saw the boat on the surface. Rowland ordered his men to stand by to ram the U-Boat, and the destroyer turned bows toward her and increased the full speed. Prien saw him coming and dived again—just in time. The destroyer sped over the spot where he had gone down, readying depth charges at shallow setting.

Now Prien had some bad luck. *U-47* ran through a patch of phosphorescence and the churning water gave Rowland a good idea of the position of the submarine. *Wolverine* fired a 10-charge pattern. One or more of the charges slammed into *U-47* and smashed her plates. The sea came pouring in then, and that was the end of Guenther Prien, the Bull of Scapa Flow. For the British it was an inconclusive victory. For hours afterward

Wolverine chased and depth charged a school of porpoises, but there was no question about the fate of *U-47*. Doenitz called all day long on March 8 for the submarine to report her position. But all he heard, from her and from *U-70*, was the deep silence of the sea.

During this attack on OB 293, Kretschmer in *U-99* and Schepke in *U-100* were also on the attack. Schepke played it safe that day and stayed out of trouble. Kretschmer found the convoy at one o'clock on the morning of March 7 and pulled his usual trick of sneaking in among the ships and "joining" them before the attack at point-blank range on the surface. He fired at what he thought was a tanker and hit her. She began sending distress signals, and he learned that he had hit *Terje Viken*, the largest whaling mother ship in the world, more than 20,000 tons! Kretschmer then torpedoed a tanker, the *Athelbeach*, and finished her off with gunfire. This took until dawn. By that time the *Wolverine* and other destroyers were moving back into the area, picking up survivors and looking for submarine prey. Kretschmer withdrew, at high speed, two corvettes after him. He watched as *U-70* dived with a corvette after her, just before he took *U-99* below. And that was the last he ever saw of *Korvettenkapitaen* Matz and the *U-70*. In a few minutes, from his hiding place under the flotsam in the sea, Kretschmer could hear the depth charging that meant attack on *U-70*. He knew, from intercepting a radio report, that Matz had already suffered a damaged conning tower in an earlier depth charge attack. And now, the corvettes were after something with a vengeance. Kretschmer was attacked too—*U-99* counted more than 100 depth charges thrown down at her, but the golden horse-shoe held good again for him, while before the day was out, *U-70* was split in two by depth charges, and only a handful of men, including Captain Matz, were saved to tell the tale.

When the depth charging had ended and the enemy surface vessels moved away, Kretschmer surfaced. The wolf pack was sharply reduced. Prien and *U-47* were gone. So were Matz and *U-70*. *Korvettenkapitaen* Eckermann in the new big *U-A* reported that he had been so badly hit by depth charges that he was turning around and going back to base.

Kretschmer and Schepke lost contact with the convoy after that, because Prien had been the official shadower, and when he was lost precious hours were wasted in trying to raise his signal. By the time Doenitz realized that *U-47* was gone, so was convoy OB 293 out of range.

So a new wolf pack was formed, this time with *Korvettenkapitaen* Lemp as a shadower. Lemp had come a long way since the day he sank the *Athenia,* and now he had one of the new boats, *U-110,* he had won promotion, and medals, and done his share of the sinking of allied ships. The convoy was one Lemp had discovered between Iceland and 61 degrees North Latitude, bound for the east, and England.

Kretschmer and Schepke joined the tail of the convoy, shadowing it during the day. Kretschmer's *U-99* was driven down several times by flying boats and escorts. Schepke's *U-100* tried to speed "around end" and get ahead of the convoy so Schepke could start off the evening with a spread of torpedoes from the bow to take several ships at once—a technique at which he was very good. The escorts sensed his presence and forced him to dive, too, and then depth charged *U-100,* but without catching her.

The convoy commander was foxy. Near Lousy Bank, he changed course, and in so doing lost Kretschmer's *U-99* for a time. But not for long.

Kretschmer did as usual—he raced in from the port beam, rushing between a pair of escorts, and attacked a tanker. His torpedo struck and the tanker went up in a sheet of flame—aviation gasoline. The flame was like a beacon, and it illuminated the silhouette of *U-99* for the escorts, which were rushing in. Kretschmer dived hurriedly, but instead of seeking escape, he "joined" the convoy, and then surfaced again. Another tanker—another flamer. He moved to another lane, hiding from the escorts behind the smoke of his latest victim, and found a third tanker. One ship, one torpedo. It worked again. Then a torpedo for a freighter, and another torpedo for another freighter. Both hit and stopped the ships. One sank immediately, the other took two more torpedoes. Then back through the convoy again, and another freighter, another torpedo. What a night's work. This ship began to break in two, tried to ram the submarine, and then sank in a cloud of smoke and steam. *U-99* raced away, between two escorts, and headed away from the convoy.

Meanwhile, the destroyers *Vanoc* and *Walker* were moving back and forth along the fringes of the convoy, trying to find the U-Boats. Their sound apparatus was not effective against a surfaced U-Boat, for the most part. During such attacks as Kretschmer's, the escorts had to rely on finding the boat on the surface, on actually seeing it. Thus they moved and fired star shells into the night. *Walker* sighted Schepke's *U-100* on the port beam of the convoy, rushed after the submarine, which dived, and then dropped a passing pattern of "ashcans." *Walker* listened, but lost contact, and moved back to the end of the convoy then to pick up survivors of the torpedoed ships.

The captain of *Walker,* Commander Donald

Macintyre, did not know it, but his depth charges had caused serious damage to Schepke's boat, and that commander felt it necessary to surface before a plate gave way and sent them to the bottom.

With a rush, *U-100* surfaced—and now a device new to the Germans came into play. It was radar. Aboard *Vanoc,* which had radar, the operator of this new detection system reported excitedly to the bridge that a pip had suddenly appeared on his screen. Submarine! *Vanoc* reported to *Walker* to the TBS, and the two destroyers turned and sped toward the pip's position. It was not long before they came upon the U-Boat surfaced, unaware in the darkness, and *Vanoc* hurtled down upon Schepke's boat in a swirl of fast water. The destroyer struck just amidships and threw all those on deck into the sea, except Captain Schepke. For him a horrible fate was waiting. The rushing destroyer pinned him in the conning tower and cut his legs off from the trunk of his body, which was jammed against the periscope sheath. The destroyer ran up onto the submarine, and then strained mightily to back off. Suddenly the bows came clear, Schepke's body was released and tossed into the sea; he moved his arms a few times, and then he sank. *U-100* rose bow high in the air, and then plunged to the bottom of the sea. Five swimmers were left struggling in the cold water, and *Vanoc* picked them up. Five men, all that were left of the crew of *U-100*.

As the destroyers concentrated on Schepke's boat, in *U-99* a triumphant Kretschmer had gone below, leaving an officer on watch in the conning tower as the submarine moved out, away from the convoy, her torpedoes gone and her night's work done. Kretschmer wrote out a message for Doenitz. He had sunk the tankers *Ferm, Bed-*

ouin, Franche Comte, and *Korsham,* and the freighters *Venetia* and *F.B. White* that night. He was pleased with himself, as he wrote.

Just then, he felt the boat diving, and the officer of watch came rushing down the ladder. What was wrong?

Destroyers. Very close. They must have seen the U-Boat said the officer of the watch, worriedly. A lookout had failed to report the enemy ship, and they had nearly run onto it. Kretschmer understood and took the boat down to 300 feet.

They had, indeed, nearly run into *Vanoc* and *Walker,* and now they were to pay for it. *Walker* made a run across the position indicated by the Asdic and dropped seven depth charges. They were tremendously effective. Gauges smashed and their liquid spilled out in the control room of the U-Boat. The depth gauge was destroyed—they had no way now of estimating their depth except by going forward into the torpedo compartment where a second gauge was located. The shock put out the lights and tossed the boat one way and then another. More depth charges. A pipe split, and water began pouring in. An oil tank sprang a leak, and the viscous oil began sloshing into the control room. They checked the forward depth gauge. They had sunk to 600 feet, far below the given depth of no return. They were making no headway, which meant they would sink deeper— and the plates would surely burst any moment.

Kretschmer gave the order to blow tanks and surface. But the valve was stuck. They sank, and sank, and sank, down to 700 feet and below. Then the valve gave, and they started up. Kretschmer wanted to level off at 200 feet, but the boat would not respond to control now and it leaped to the surface, bow bouncing high into the air, and then falling back. The destroyer moved in then, and circled, firing on the surfaced U-Boat.

Kretschmer went up on deck, moved his men into the protection of one side, and casually lighted a cigar. Below, the hatches were opened, and the wounded submarine began to sink. The men slid into the water, the boat slid down stern first, trapping the engineer who had gone below to flood the ballast tanks, and then she sank. But the destroyers saved all but three men of the crew, and they went to prison camp for the rest of the war.

The loss to Germany was so immense that it was weeks before Hitler would let the navy release the fact that Kretschmer and Schepke were gone, and even longer before the truth would leak out about Prien, the national hero who had sunk the *Royal Oak*. For with this grim knowledge, even Germans could not help but know that something was happening out in the Atlantic that was not to Nazi liking.

The U-Boat corps was stunned. The trio had been regarded as indestructible, and this news warned others that the good days of 1940 were gone forever. The stalking game of the Atlantic was now indeed a game of life and death for all concerned and no longer a turkey shoot for the submarines.

With their passing, techniques and controls began to change. There was less of the individual "ace" atmosphere about the U-Boats and more Doenitz precision, more danger, and less of the bravado of the buccaneer which had characterized the early operations. The story of *U-557,* one of the Atlantic boats, illustrates the new ways very well.

The captain of *U-557* was *Oberleutnant* Ottokar Paulssen, a stocky blond veteran of the U-Boat corps, although he was only in his thirties. For seven months in 1940 and 1941 the boat was in the Baltic with her four officers, three warrant officers, and 14 petty officers, and 27 seamen. After a refit at Koenigsberg, she sailed in the middle of April on trials and nearly came to grief on her way to Kiel. She was making a practice dive when the head valve jammed and she rushed to the bottom, nearly 400 feet below the surface, and hung there, her stern stuck in the mud, the 50-ton storage batteries leaking acid that sent chlorine gas through the boat. One man died from the fumes in the diesel room. The engine rooms flooded, and the whole crew escaped up into the torpedo rooms forward to try to rebalance the boat and get the stern up so they could surface. They bailed the water out of the boat with a bucket brigade, working for 14 hours. Finally they were able to equalize the weight and the boat dropped to the bottom on an even keel. Still they had to get up and get 40 tons of water out of the boat doing so. They shot compressed air into the buoyancy tanks; they surged back and forth in the boat to break the suction of the mud. Finally, after 20 hours of unremitting effort and strain, they saved the U-Boat and themselves and got to the surface. An inspection showed that someone had left a wrench in the inboard air induction valve and, of course, it had jammed the first time they tried to dive. In the shipyards and the naval stations the pressure was on these days; *U-557* had just gotten a taste of it.

The submarine was put back in the Kiel yard for an overhaul, and on May 13 it sailed. *U-557* had a fresh coat of gray paint, and 14 electric torpedoes with new, carefully modified magnetic detonators, and ammunition for her deck gun and anti-aircraft gun. She carried food for an eight-week cruise.

She sailed as part of a pack of three submarines up to the Shetland Islands, and then west into the Atlantic. Seventy miles north of the

Shetlands the ship encountered a freighter and attacked. Two torpedoes brought the lone ship down, attacked without warning, for this was the way of the new U-boat war. It was four o'clock in the morning when the lifeboats were broken out from the ship and the crew escaped in them, neither helped nor hindered by the men of *U-557*. That too was the new way.

Life aboard the U-Boat was not very pleasant. These boats were built for work not convenience of the crews. There were half enough bunks for the men; they used the "hot bunk" method, in which the man not on watch slept, then went on watch and his bunk-mate took over the warm bed. The moisture condensed on the bulkheads and then ran down into the bilges in wet slimy streaks. Food turned rotten in the humidity and had to be thrown overboard. The fresh bread they brought from shore lasted about a week, then mold set in. Life on the surface was rough; the boat pitched and tossed in the almost continual wind of the North Atlantic. Only the daily trim dive brought relief, and then, below the surface, the boat was calm and peaceful and if they did not stay down long even the stink was not bad.

U-557 was on her way to her patrol area. Long since she had lost contact with the other wolves of her pack, but that would be remedied later. Now, on May 25, she encountered a convoy of 30 ships, just before sunset, and prepared to attack them.

Paulssen had his own technique. His executive officer did the firing of the torpedoes, and they went out in spreads, like fans. This night they surfaced ahead of the convoy and prepared for a shot. But then Paulssen saw that the escorts were off somewhere on the flanks, and he slipped into the convoy himself, in a manner reminiscent of Otto Kretschmer. He steered between the columns and ordered the exec to shoot on both sides.

The executive officer fired one, two, three, four, five torpedoes. The first fish hit a ship to starboard. The second hit to port. The third hit still another ship, and in a few moments all three of them broke up and sank, burning furiously. But five torpedoes had been too many, two of them were wasted, because when the first ship exploded, the alert convoy commander turned the whole fleet sharply away, and those last torpedoes missed clean. It was one of the disadvantages of the fan attack as opposed to Kretschmer's one ship, one torpedo system.

As demanded, Captain Paulssen reported to Doenitz, but instead of congratulations he received a sharp order to stop his single-handed attack and shadow this convoy until Doenitz could bring the rest of the wolf pack up to do a really destructive job. Paulssen was furious, but probably no angrier than Doenitz, who did not like to have his submarine commanders going off on their own hook.

Actually, this attitude of Doenitz' represented no more than prudence these days, with the new development in British defensive measures. This day, *U-557* had a taste of what the allies called the hunter-killer group method of defense against U-Boats. Paulssen had scarcely finished his transmission when the lookout on watch shouted that a destroyer was coming in on them at less than 3000 yards, a bone in her teeth, and headed straight for the conning tower. Then came another, and another! Three escorts which seemed to know precisely where the U-Boat was, even in the darkness. Paulssen turned, right full rudder, and ran into the sea, hoping that his low silhouette would be blotted out. But the British had radar as well as Asdic, and they turned with the submarine and followed, closing the gap, for they could make a good 10 knots more than the U-Boat.

The captain saw and gave the alarm. The siren screeched through the boat, and she began to dive as the watch clambered down into the conning tower hatch and dogged the door behind them. Down they went, swiftly, to 500 feet, hoping to escape the depth charging. But the British knew. There was a click, and then a crash, and a shock that lifted the submarine as if picked up bodily and flung down again. The lights went out. She dropped another 40 feet.

The boat chief called for emergency lights. They blew the tanks and raised the diving planes to get the ship on an even keel, and they rigged for silent running to keep *U-557* from sinking. All other motors were shut off. The men virtually held their breaths. And they waited.

The explosions shook the boat, so close as to be terrifying. Then, Paulssen realized that he was under attack by at least two escorts and he took desperate measures, knowing that they were just that. The submarine's lines of defense underwater were depth and silence. He had the depth; he was further lucky in that it was an extremely stormy day and the surface attackers were hampered even in their listening by the weather. But Paulssen also felt this was not enough and his proof was the nearness of the depth charges. So he risked everything and ordered full speed on both electric motors, chancing the noise in order to change his position drastically and quickly.

Three more depth charges came very close, then they moved away—or rather the submarine moved away at right angles to her old position and lost the pursuers. Now it was a question of keeping from being found again—and Paulssen ran for three hours submerged before he felt it was safe to blow the boat and come to the surface. He then headed back in the direction last taken by the convoy to do the job Doenitz had assigned him.

To the German naval mind there were matters even more important than convoys, and this day of May 27, *U-557* learned of one of them. The battleship *Bismarck* was at sea, and she was beleaguered by an entrapping British force. At headquarters Doenitz was alerted and ordered all U-Boats with torpedoes to proceed to the aid of the battleship. It was a forlorn gesture—*U-557* abandoned her chase of the convoy and did as told but had to travel 350 miles, and even by speeding on the surface arrived on the scene so late that all she found was an area of water covered with oil and debris, not a raft, not a man. It had all been futile.

So Paulssen reported and then prepared to move, responding to orders Doenitz gave from the plotting room, where he kept his military chessboard of the Atlantic. For communication and navigation purposes Doenitz had marked off the Atlantic into grid squares. Thus with four symbols he could order a submarine to a specific area, and now he sent *U-557* to square AK50 with the promise that a convoy was heading that way, moving north-northeast at a speed of nine knots. The order meant that one of Doenitz' other boats had spotted the convoy and was doing the shadowing job. *U-557* had just received the pack call, and as she sped toward the scene, Paulssen knew that other U-Boats—every one capable of making the area in time—were being sent to join the pack.

Doenitz depended on "Intelligence" for his operations, and he was remarkably hampered during the war because Field Marshal Herman Goering did not like him and would not cooperate reasonably with the submarine force by making adequate aerial observation units available. For a time, Hitler himself forced Goering to give Doenitz a certain amount of support from big planes capable of reaching far out in the Atlantic, but it was always done grudgingly, and except in the waters around the coast and in the north, air was not a very important part of the operation. Certainly in the Atlantic it never reached its potential. Doenitz also relied to some extent on Admiral Canaris and his naval Intelligence group, but again the submarine commander and the Intelligence officer did not get on well, which did not help matters. Thus many times the intelligence that Doenitz had about convoys and ship movements was sketchy or even faulty. So it was this time. *U-557* sped toward her assigned position and began working across it like a sock darner. But after many hours, Paulssen had to radio Doenitz that he had found nothing. So Doenitz sent him to another square to intercept a convoy which was supposed to pass 600 miles south of Greenland. Intelligence from Canada reported that the convoy had assembled outside the Halifax harbor and was going to move.

Paulssen headed for his new square. On the way he found a "loner," a fast, modern freighter that had chosen to brave the dangers of the Atlantic by herself. She took two torpedoes, and then sank.

With only five torpedoes left, *U-557* hastened to do Doenitz' bidding and moved toward mid-Atlantic. She was also low on fuel. But in the middle of 1941, Doenitz had made special provisions for his wolf packs in order to obviate the need for return every eight weeks to resupply. Now *U-557* was ordered to rendezvous with the tanker *Belchen* off the coast of Greenland, and she headed to the designated position. En route

she encountered three British warships and dis-
creetly submerged and watched them pass. Life
was changing in mid-Atlantic. Then she went on.

When *U-557* found the tanker, she and three
other U-Boats filled their fuel compartments. They
took food, and now, with the exception of the
torpedo shortage, were ready to work all over
again. But it was another measure of the changing scene in the Atlantic that almost immediately after they left the rendezvous with *Belchen*
the men of *U-557* heard the noise of explosions
and firing from her direction. And later they
learned that the British warships had found the
tanker and had destroyed her that day. They did
so even as one of the boats, *U-93*, was still fuel-
ing, and while the U-Boat saved itself and came
up to rescue the crew of *Belchen*, it was a serious
reverse for Doenitz, one of a series, as the British
navy scoured the seas for the surface ships that
fed the wolf packs.

On this patrol, *U-557* then moved to the 47th
parallel to search the convoy route between Halifax and St. John's. They went on station and
cruised slowly, on the surface, one day after the
next. One evening they were abruptly attacked
by a British submarine, which fired three torpedoes at them—but missed because the torpedoes
ran too deep and passed beneath the submarine.
They chased the other (probably it was out of
torpedoes and had to run away) and when the
British ship surfaced they saw it was a *Thames*
class submarine. But they could not come to grips
with it and stopped the chase soon after.

It was June 23 before the *U-557* had new instructions, which involved the suspected presence of another convoy, some 22 hours sailing
time from her position. Paulssen headed for the
assigned area, mindful of the orders from Doenitz:
the first U-Boat to make contact must report

location and speed before attacking. It was Doenitz' great problem that his U-Boat captains were loath to do his bidding. They saw the war from their perspective as a series of actions, not as he saw it, as a movement and concentration of forces. In this case, U-Boat commander Paulssen could not contain himself. There *was* a convoy; he came upon it and immediately prepared to shoot. But he did restrain himself long enough to follow orders, even as he was moving to attack position, and radio to Doenitz.

Even as *U-557* launched her first torpedoes two escorts were bearing down on her—an indication of the rapidly bettering state of British radar and other defenses. She shot and immediately submerged, dived to escape the rain of depth charges that must fall. She fired three torpedoes, and two of them exploded, but what happened to the ships *U-557* was not to know, because she did not get her head up again to see the convoy. The leisurely days of Kretschmer, Prien, and Schepke were long behind the U-Boat corps. *U-557* dived deep, well below 500 feet, and was saved that day by her depth. Three escorts came after her. The depth charges damaged the starboard motor, sprang a leak in the diesel compartment, and caused the rudder to jam. Instruments were broken, and half the ship's crockery was destroyed. The plates in the deck jumped with each explosion, the lights went out. The gaskets sprang leaks, and the bilges filled with water.

U-557 was saved that day primarily because of the message to Doenitz. In time the escorts moved away, called by the need to protect the convoy from the other ships of the wolf pack. From below, the men of Paulssen's submarine could hear the smashing impact of torpedoes, and then they were left alone as the escorts rushed off like firemen to put out a new blaze. After several

hours of silence, the U-boat surfaced and the
crew examined the damage. The starboard motor
had been knocked off its foundation. A ballast
tank was ruptured and a propeller shaft bent.
She was very lucky indeed, and fit only to limp
homeward, 1600 miles to the French coast. She
had sunk an estimated 37,000 tons of British
shipping—but now even the estimates were becoming suspect because the U-Boats seldom had
a chance to observe their victims very closely.
The battle of the Atlantic changed every day.

The German high command moved a number
of U-Boats into the South Atlantic this summer,
and they enjoyed more success against convoys
coming from South America and Africa. Seven
U-Boats sank 74 ships in a short time. The British changed the convoy routes and increased the
defenses by air and by sea, and in the last months
of 1941 the changes showed in the sinkings. The
U-Boats were still successful; it was a matter of
degree. They were encountering much more
opposition.

There were huge success stories, as that of
convoy SC 42, from which the U-Boat wolf pack
sank 16 ships on September 11 and would have
sunk many more had not a change in the weather
brought fog and safety to the convoy the next
day. Another convoy coming from Freetown that
month lost seven of 11 ships to the wolves. Doenitz
was hampered however by several factors. One
was the need to split forces in North and South
Atlantic. One was the need to cover a new area—
with the march of the Germans into Russia. One
was a demand by the high command that he
move submarines into the Mediterranean to support the operations of General Rommel in Africa.
And then, the British defenses on the sea were
nothing to sneeze at these days. The case of raider
Atlantis was a good indication.

Atlantis—Raider 16—was a converted merchantman which had terrorized the southern seas for a
year and a half, sinking 22 ships on her voyage,
and left alone she might have kept at it. But
Doenitz' needs were very great for supply of his
submarines. Germany had no bases, no friends
outside Europe who would help her, and away
from home her submarines must feed from ships.
So *Raider 16* was sent into the South Atlantic to
give oil and food to German U-Boats, a very
dangerous task, because the British were searching hard for these supply ships. On schedule,
Captain Bernhard Rogge met U-Boat *U-126* south
of the equator, and they hooked up so *Atlantis*
could refuel the submarine. Rogge had already
refuelled *U-68*, some 500 miles southwest of St.
Helena, and although her captain quite agreed
with him that it was dangerous work (and Rogge
thought it was also unnecessary and wasteful
use of his ship), it had to be done Doenitz' way.
And so on the morning of November 22, *Raider
16* and the *U-126* were caught on the surface by
the British cruiser *Devonshire,* just as *Kapitaenleutnant* Bauer, the captain of the U-Boat, was
talking about taking a real bath aboard the raider.
The U-Boat crash dived and escaped without her
captain. *Raider 16* was sunk by the guns of the
Devonshire, leaving 300 men struggling in the
water. The submarine surfaced, and by using life
rafts and rubber boats, managed to help save the
survivors until the U-Boat supply ship *Python*
could come to the rescue. *Python* was designated
by Doenitz as the tender and supply ship for the
U-Boats *U-A, U-124, U-68,* and *U-129.* She saved
the crew of *Atlantis,* and then went to a rendezvous where she was to meet her U-Boats and
refuel them. But she was found by HMS *Dorsetshire,*
another British cruiser, and in spite of the presence of three German submarines, *Python* was

sunk and *Dorsetshire* steamed away, not taking
prisoners because she was wary of the U-Boats.
And then there were 500 men struggling in the
sea. Soon, four U-Boats had assembled to help
the stricken seamen. *U-A, U-68, U-121,* and
U-129 all came to assist. Four Italian submarines came up. They were the *Tazzoli,* the *Finzi,*
the *Calvi,* and the *Torelli.* And together, the submarines brought the survivors of the surface ships
back to safety in Germany. But it was scarcely
the satisfactory way to use submarines, and it
showed Doenitz that he would have to change his
tactics to use tanker submarines for his supply.
And there were other indications of change. In
December, a wolf pack attacked a British convoy
bound northward from Gibraltar to discover that
the convoy was protected by an aircraft carrier.
This carrier was sunk by a submarine, but only
two merchantmen went down, and in the operation the Germans lost five U-Boats. The combination of air power and new escorts and experience
was working against the U-Boats. Then came
December 7, 1941.

CHAPTER FIVE

The Broadening War

Doenitz' campaign to get more and better U-Boats was successful in a way, but the trouble was that the war kept getting bigger as his U-Boat force increased. He had wanted a force of 300 submarines to fight England. By the end of 1941 he had about 250 U-Boats but he had two new wars to fight, and because of the battering nature of the struggles, only 91 of his boats were operational. Then came the declaration of war against the United States, and Doenitz had a whole new problem.

From the positive point of view for the Germans at least wraps were off. For many months the U-Boats had been forbidden to operate in the ship-infested waters off the United States, but now they could go anywhere and sink just about anything they saw. There had been previous encounters with American warships, and they had been very frustrating to the U-Boat men. The battleship *Texas* had appeared in the sights of *U-203*, and her captain had suggested that he might attack. Doenitz had responded with a horrified order to lay off and followed that with a policy directive which came straight from the Fuhrer, forbidding any attacks on American ships.

In September, the American destroyer *Greer* had shadowed *U-652* for hours, not attacking but warning all the ships at sea of her presence and inviting a British warship to come and attack. Finally, after several hours of this harassment, *U-652* had broken Doenitz' rules and fired two torpedoes at the American destroyer. Luckily for the captain of the submarine both had missed, because Hitler would have had his head, even though *Greer* had depth charged the submarine after the attack. Two American ships had actually been sunk: the USS *Kearny* and the USS *Reuben James.* But the pretense of "neutral" relations had been maintained until the end of 1941.

Immediately after the declaration of war, Doenitz was able to divert five U-Boats to American waters, and they began to sail just before Christmas. First to go was *U-123,* whose captain was *Kapitaenleutnant* Richard Hardegan, and she was off the coast of the United States at the end of the first week of January. But the operation was not to begin until Doenitz ordered it, and he wanted the sinkings to start on January 13. So Hardegan cruised along the Canadian coast, and on January 11 he was stalking. Next day he sank the British freighter *Cyclops.* The operation that Doenitz called *Paukenschlage* (downbeat) had begun.

On the night of January 13, *U-123* was off the southern tip of Long Island, just 60 miles offshore, when the lookouts aboard the submarine reported a ship. The submarine torpedoed her, and then learned that she was the tanker *Norness* and that she thought she had struck a mine. *That* captain was quickly disabused because *U-123* put a second torpedo into her.

The sinking of the *Norness* caused the American naval forces to put its first anti-submarine patrol at work—and what a sad little squadron it was. It consisted of a destroyer, a coast guard cutter, a minesweeper, a blimp, and a handful of planes. They went out manfully, but they did not find the submarine.

Meanwhile Captain Hardegan sank the British tanker *Coimbra* just 20 miles off Southampton, and then headed south to Cape Hatteras. On January 17, he sank the tanker *Allen Jackson* just off the lightship of Diamond Shoals. Then he sank the freighter *Norvana*. A day later he sank *City of Atlanta*. He was low on torpedoes and came across eight ships all travelling with their lights on. He shelled the tanker *Malay,* then sank the freighter *Ciltvaria,* and went back and spent his last torpedo sinking the *Malay,* which had made the mistake of telling the world she was still afloat after the shelling and was heading for Norfolk.

Then *U-123* headed for home.

But into American waters came the other submarines of the special force sent out by Doenitz. *U-66* sank five ships, and the other three submarines sank more, totalling nearly 100,000 tons of shipping. Before the end of January the Americans certainly knew that there was a war on in the Atlantic. In two months the Germans sank 600,000 tons of ships off the American coast and in the Caribbean. By the first of August they had sunk 519 ships in these waters and the oil was actually fouling the beaches of the eastern coast of the United States.

By the end of the year more than 1000 allied ships were lost, and when the authorities explained it in terms of the war effort, it was a very serious loss indeed: the loss of a freighter of average size was the equivalent of losing 300 freight cars full of goods. The Germans had found a new fertile field for the use of the U-Boats, and while the British had learned how to counteract them, the same could not be said for the American navy at that point. In the summer of 1942 General George Marshall, chief of staff of the army, said that he feared the submarine menace was threatening the entire American war effort. And the strange fact was that all this havoc was wreaked by a handful of submarines, perhaps a dozen on station at any given time. In three months the U-Boats accounted for 1,200,000 tons of ships, and Doenitz only lost one boat in the operations. The American defenses were so feeble that the Nazis were contemptuous of them. But as for the British, they were now very much to be feared. They had developed a new short wave radar, and Doenitz began to feel its effects. In February, March, and April, three submarines were lost under strange circumstances. In February, *U-82* reported that she had sighted a small convoy west of the Bay of Biscay and was going to attack. Then her transmissions ceased. She was lost. In March, one day, *U-587* made the same kind of report. She disappeared. In April, *U-252* reported such a convoy, and Doenitz urged him to extreme caution. But this boat, too, disappeared. Doenitz began to believe the British were running a special anti-submarine convoy with trick weapons—but it was not so. British defenses were simply becoming a match for the U-Boats.

As for the American station, however, Doenitz was still riding high. The first submarine tanker, *U-459*, was ready for action in the spring of 1942, and she went to the American area to make it possible for the smaller U-Boats to stay longer on station. When the American defenses were concentrated in the north, the Germans moved to the area of Key West. Then in April, the Americans adopted the convoy system off the eastern coast, and the sinkings went up. Doenitz was remarkably responsive to the changes in conditions and able to move his slender force of U-Boats very swiftly. Here, too, when the convoy system was introduced, the losses went down remarkably; Doenitz went back to the wolf-pack techniques.

But the halcyon period was over, partly because Hitler was making so many demands on the U-Boat force. In the spring of 1942 one of those demands concerned northern waters. Hitler had the idea that the British were going to invade Norway, and he also wanted to prevent convoys from reaching Soviet Russia over the Murmansk run. So he ordered Doenitz to detail 20 U-Boats to northern waters. The order came as a tremendous shock to Doenitz, who was just getting ready to concentrate anew on the North American runway. But orders were orders. And from this order of Hitler's sprang a new sea war that was almost indescribably awesome, in which hunter and hunted were both the prey of the most dangerous of elements—cold. Men of the allied and Nazi navies both hated the northern run, but it was war and for reasons they were not to question the run must be made.

The Russian convoys began in 1941, from British waters to the best and most open ports of Russia that could be found. Chief among these was Murmansk, at the head of the Kola Inlet, some 200 miles east of the North Cape in Norway. Murmansk is free of ice all year around, so most convoys came here. They much preferred to go to Archangel, 400 miles southeast of Murmansk, but the Archangel area could be kept open in winter only by ice breakers, and not *always*, either. They faced a multiplicity of dangers: the German pocket battleships and cruisers, destroyers, German aircraft, and the U-Boats. The PQ series of convoys started from Britain in late September, 1941, and they braved all these dangers. PQ 1 even had an uneventful passage and reached Russia on October 11 without a loss. By the end of the year 53 loaded ships had reached Russia and still none had been lost. That was when Hitler began to get the wind up. The *Tirpitz* went out to search for allied ships, and the *Hipper* was also dispatched to northern waters. And so were the submarines.

The beginning of the period was unlucky for Doenitz. *U-655* was sunk in March by a British minesweeper as she tracked the 19-ship convoy from Russia to England that was called QP9. Convoy PQ 13, going *to* Russia, was attacked by three destroyers and a German submarine wolf pack. Two ships were torpedoed but the destroyer *Fury* sank *U-585*. Doenitz was not happy. His spirits picked up in April, when *U-456* managed to put two torpedoes into the cruiser *Edinburgh* as that British ship escorted convoy QP 11 on its way home. One fish hit the cruiser amidships and the other hit in the after portion, blowing off her stern and rudder. *U-456* then shadowed the helpless cruiser as she was trying to make port, protected by British and Russian destroyers, but it was German destroyers that finished off the cruiser. Even so Doenitz was quite convinced by mid-summer 1942 that these extreme northern waters were unsuitable for U-Boat attack because of the shortness of the summer nights, which deprived the submarines of the surprise factor. Then came a convoy known as PQ 17.

The Germans were waiting for this convoy. The *Luftwaffe* had 264 airplanes ready to strike. The *Tirpitz* and the *Admiral Hipper* were to be unleashed. And Doenitz' U-Boats were ready. Here was a chance, they said in Berlin, to wipe out a whole convoy, down to the last ship. Having broken the British naval codes, the Germans knew how and when the convoy was coming. They had extra time, too, because PQ 17 was scheduled to sail earlier, but demands on the British for escorts to Malta had been such that it had been delayed. That gave the Germans extra time to prepare.

Doenitz allocated 12 of his 20 northern submarines to the convoy destruction force. Early in June, when German agents reported that PQ 17 was forming off the southwest coast of Iceland, *U-251, U-376,* and *U-408* were sent to the Denmark Strait to watch. This was to be a combined operation so they were to have a new task. They were to shadow the convoy—much more important than launching an attack at the beginning. So this group, called the Ice Devil Pack, set out.

German Intelligence reported that PQ 17 was a huge convoy and that it would reach Mayen Island around June 20. The place to attack was east of Bear Island, between 20 and 30 degrees East Longitude. Battleships, destroyers, planes, and submarines were ready. On June 16 more submarines headed out from Norway. *U-657, U-88, U-355, U-334, U-457, U-255, U-456*—all were sent to join the Ice Devil Pack. And later two more submarines, *U-657* and *U-703,* would be dispatched for this fight.

They waited at sea.

The convoy was supposed to come, but it did not come, and the U-Boat crews fretted as their boats patrolled south of Jan Mayen Island.

Meanwhile the convoy ships delayed at Iceland. As the Germans knew what the Americans and British were planning, so did allied Intelligence learn that the Germans were, on their side, preparing for a major engagement at sea, using their battleships against this convoy. They, too, would use big ships, including the *Duke of York,* the flagship of Admiral Tovey, commander in chief of the Home Fleet, and the American battleship *Washington,* flagship of American Rear Admiral R. C. Giffen, commander of Task Force 99.

And now PQ 17 got a new purpose; it was not only to be a convoy of some 30 big ships, carrying war materials from the U.S. to Russia, but it was to be a trap for the German navy, to catch the Nazis' heavy ships.

So PQ 17 sailed on the afternoon of June 17 from Hvalfiord in Iceland; 35 ships, carrying tanks, heavy guns, and bombers for the Russians. In all there were 297 planes, 594 tanks, 4246 trucks, and 156,000 tons of ammunition, medical supplies, and all the other needs of an army. It was estimated that this convoy carried the material to supply an army of 50,000 men.

The first ship to be lost to the convoy was the *Richard Bland,* which ran aground on the rocks and had to return to port. She left, and the convoy formed itself into nine columns, protected at this early, noncritical point by three minesweepers and four anti-submarine trawlers, also by two oilers which would serve the escorts and three rescue ships. They were joined later by two British submarines and a corvette, the *Dianella.*

On June 30, a four-engined Focke-Wulf found the convoy and informed German naval headquarters in Norway. Late in the afternoon so did *Korvettenkapitaen* Max-Martin Teichert in *U-456.* He did not have a chance to report, however, because he was almost immediately forced to dive by the escorts, and then was subjected to depth charging. So the submarine report was made by *Korvettenkapitaen* Reinhard Reche in *U-255* about four o'clock that afternoon.

Headquarters now ordered the U-Boats to the area, and they went. What weather they found! It was cloudy and overcast, the sky was gray

What they could do. A warship lies with her back broken after torpedoing by one of Admiral Doenitz' U-Boats.

The *U-3008*, one of the new Type XXI U-Boats in production at the very end of World War II. This boat was capable of extremely long voyages completely underwater. Had it been in production a year earlier, it might have made a great deal of difference in the outcome of the sea war.

A stricken U-Boat, victim of air attack, burns in the Atlantic.

Such small aircraft carriers as this "jeep" carrier joined the allied convoys in 1943 and made all the difference in the world in the war against the U-Boats.

On watch. Lookouts on the bridge of a U-Boat in the Atlantic.

Now hear this... American sailors and German U-Boat captives aboard the deck of a carrier in the Atlantic.

A near miss. An American bomber goes after a U-Boat in mid-Atlantic.

A sort of bath. German U-Boat prisoners of war get a hosing down to remove some of the oil after their capture in mid-Atlantic.

Survivors of a ship sunk by the U-Boat come alongside for directions and whatever else they can get.

Relaxing a bit. A big U-Boat on the surface.

Prehistoric monster? No, it is the snorkel of a U-Boat.

Admiral Daniel Gallery's USS *Guadalcanal* came upon the *U-505* at sea one day in 1945, and this was the result. The Nazi ship became an American submarine.

The skipper's quarters of the *U-505*. This was also the wardroom.

The German submarine crew with their American captor.

A German U-Boat skipper and part of his crew in the North Atlantic in winter.

Admiral Doenitz congratulates a young U-Boat crewman decorated for bravery.

Control room of a U-Boat.

Coming into port was always a happy occasion.

A nice pattern of depth charges surrounds what the destroyermen hope is a U-Boat.

Every bit of the space aboard a U-Boat had its purpose. Note the clothing hanging down beside the depth gauge of this U-Boat.

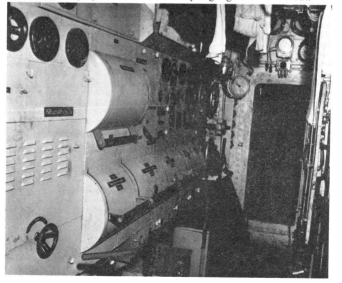

A happy skipper on a good day.

The snorkel.

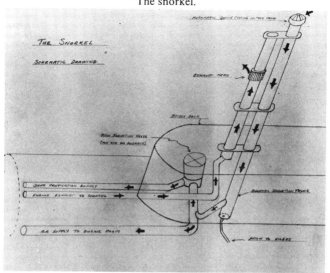

Gallery of a U-Boat.

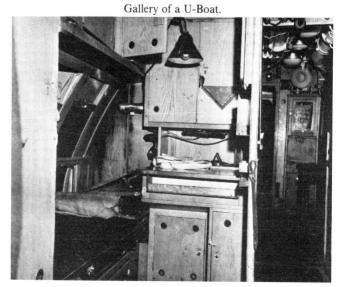

Shifting torpedoes at sea was always a dangerous job.

Lt. Comdr. Guenther Prien, the "Bull of Scapa Flow," who sank the British battleship *Royal Oak*.

U-744, sunk by a British frigate.

The U-Boat skippers were ardent and very young, and most of them cared nothing for Nazi politics.

One of Doenitz' boys with his bride. Most of the U-Boat captains did not survive the war. The casualties in the force were 85 percent, the highest in any service.

and so was the sea, and all was covered with huge patches of fog that made visibility totally haphazard. Several of the submarines were on the fringe of the convoy, but they had no chance to attack. The escorts were busy, and their depth charging kept the submarines down below the surface that afternoon. That evening the U-Boats were ordered to their duty. Three of them were to shadow the convoy. The other six in the immediate area were to set up a patrol line ahead of the convoy and wait. The German naval commander in Norway, Admiral Hubert Schmundt, sent the message. The Germans, however, were not the only ones who had broken codes—so had the British broken German naval code—and so each side had a good idea of what the other was actually doing, although, of course, not of the precise enemy plans.

On July 1, the German warships in Norwegian ports were ready to sail against the convoy. By the morning of July 2, the weather had turned particularly foul, very foggy, and the U-Boats had to move so close to the convoy to see it or sense it with their hydrophones that they were continually arousing the escorts, which then pursued them. The game was very wearying for the U-Boat crews.

The first attack was made by *U-255* that afternoon. She came in and launched two torpedoes from outside the escort screen. The American ship *Bellingham* was the target. She saw the torpedo tracks and turned hard to starboard. The torpedoes missed. In rushed the escorts and began dropping their depth charges.

When Admiral Schmundt learned of the attack, he was not pleased. He ordered the submarines to leave the convoy alone. They must wait.

The German air force began its attacks on the afternoon of July 2, coming in with torpedo bombers. The ships of the convoy raised barrage balloons to harry the attackers. The result was one ship shot up by cannon fire from the planes, and the loss of one German bomber, which crashed into the sea. But that evening the *Tirpitz* and the cruiser *Hipper* sailed.

Now the activity began in earnest. All night long the escorts chased one submarine after another. *Korvettenkapitaen* Heino Bohmann in *U-88* had raced all day to get ahead of the convoy, then come in and make an attack. Once he surfaced, just ahead—and found a destroyer looking down his throat. He turned and raced ahead again, and surfaced, and found another destroyer coming after him. By the time he came back to periscope depth, the convoy had passed over, the weather had closed in so that visibility was no better than 200 yards, and he had lost contact.

In *U-355 Fregattenkapitaen* Gunther La Baume was sighted by a corvette, which charged down on him and depth charged him. He dived, just in time, and escaped the six depth charges, but then lost the convoy. By midnight it was swallowed in the mist and there was quiet.

Next morning the U-Boats found the convoy again, but now they had a new problem: several of them were running low on fuel and would have to break off soon and return to base. They continued to shadow on July 3 and tried to close in for attack, but the weather was too bad and the vigilance of the escorts too great. All day long the sound of depth charging surrounded the convoy as the escorts kept the U-Boats down.

That night came first blood for the aircraft. A Heinkel torpedo bomber "got" one Liberty ship. He torpedoed the *Christopher Newport*, which slowed and was then abandoned. Hours later *U-457* came upon her, sitting lifeless in the sea, and sank her with a torpedo. So German planes and submarines shared the honor of the first kill.

The bombers attacked heavily on July 4 and hit three merchant ships, but one of them, the Russian tanker *Azerbaijan,* repaired the damage and rejoined the convoy. *Korvettenkapitaen* Hilmar Siemon in *U-334* came upon the other two, the *Navarino* and the *William Hooper* later, as they lay dead in the water. He fired a torpedo at *Navarino,* which chose to sink just before the torpedo hit. He fired two torpedoes at *William Hooper,* which broke up and sank. The crews of both ships had been taken off by rescue vessels.

The convoy was scattered, a situation the U-Boats liked very much. They now began to hunt in seriousness. In *U-703 Korvettenkapitaen* Heinz Bielfield attacked the British *Empire Byron,* a 6000-ton steamer, carrying tanks to Russia. The U-Boat launched two torpedoes from a range of two miles. Both missed, going ahead of her—a miscalculation of the ship's speed. Bielfield fired two more torpedoes, and they missed. He then swung around to make a stern shot, and this torpedo hit the ship in the engine room. She began to settle. Twenty minutes later her boiler exploded as the men were getting over the side in boats and rafts. Of the crew 42 survived, but 18 died, and the ship went down.

Captain Bielfield then surfaced and moved among the lifeboats. He lectured the British captain and crew against fighting for the communists. An army captain who had been going to teach the Russians how to use British tanks was captured and kept aboard the submarine. The others were directed to land, 250 miles away, and the U-Boat men gave them some sausage and apple juice, then *U-703* submerged.

In another part of the convoy, *U-88* was tracking the ship *Carlton,* which was carrying tanks, ammunition, and 200 tons of TNT. Captain Bohmann was submerged. He came to periscope depth, saw his quarry, waited until she moved into the crosswires of the periscope, and fired from 600 yards—two torpedoes.

Half a minute later there was a clang as the first torpedo struck the side of the ship—and then so violent an explosion, shaded in black smoke, that Bohmann could not understand what had happened. He fired another torpedo, even as the crew was getting off the wounded *Carlton*. It ran around the ship in circles, just missing the rafts and lifeboats. A seaman tried to hit it with an oar. Luckily he missed, and then the torpedo sank. Bohmann waited and watched at periscope depth. He was ready to use another torpedo. But at 10:50 on the morning of July 5, the ship rolled over and sank.

That day brought the bombers again, even as the submarines continued the chase. Bombers hit the American ship *Daniel Morgan*, which was carrying steel, food, cars, tanks, and high explosives. The crew abandoned. Bohmann came up in *U-88* and sank her with a pair of torpedoes. He surfaced and asked the Americans in the boats what their ship had been carrying. Leather and general cargo, they lied. He did not believe them, but there was nothing to be done. He gave directions to land and then set off on the surface after the convoy.

Siemon's *U-334* now closed on the American freighter *Honomu;* the captain took careful aim and fired three torpedoes. Nothing happened. He turned and fired a stern torpedo, and even as he did so, the ship's side exploded. What had happened? He could not understand—until he surfaced, and just then another submarine, *U-456,* came up almost alongside. Teichert had fired the torpedoes that hit the ship and sank her—the

U-Boats were running all over themselves in this wolf pack. And if that were not quite enough company, along now came *U-88* and surfaced. Teichert then captured the captain of the ship and took him aboard the submarine for interrogation, and the three submarines moved off on the surface together.

PQ 17's American merchant ships were not precisely tigers. Seeing the *Daniel Morgan* go down, the crew of the American Liberty ship *Samuel Chase* actually abandoned their ship although they had not been bombed or torpedoed. They sat in the lifeboats for two hours, 600 yards off their ship, and waited for torpedoes to hit her. And only after two hours did they go back aboard and resume their voyage.

On the afternoon of July 5 the German bombers were at work again, and they set the steamer *Peter Kerr* afire; she burned and blew up. They bombed *Bolton Castle*, which was carrying explosives, and she exploded like a Roman candle. They bombed the freighter *Washington*, and she burned. The rescue ship *Zaafaran* sank.

The submarine packs came back, and *U-334* and *U-456* sank the cargo ship *Earlston*. They captured the captain and put him below in *U-334* and then steamed off, the U-Boat captains talking and congratulating each other on the good hunting as they went.

U-334 was attacked very shortly thereafter while on the surface—by a JU 88—a German airplane. The plane came in and bombed before anyone saw it and jammed her steering gear so she could not submerge. Headquarters ordered her home then and also told *U-456* to escort the submarine back to Norway. She started back, along with *U-456* and another boat, *U-657*, which had sprung a leak in a fuel tank.

Four more boats were left in this particular

area, all of them reporting that they were chasing single merchant ships. Bombers harried the *Pankraft*, and her crew abandoned her not long afterward. She burned for 24 hours and blew up on the morning of July 7 with a noise so loud that she was heard even by the rest of the convoy far away.

U-703 torpedoed *River Afton*, another steamer, and when she did not sink quickly hit her again, even as the members of the crew were trying to rescue some members of the black gang who were trapped below. The second torpedo killed the men below decks, and dozens of men were thrown struggling into the cold water. Captain Bielfield was still impatient because the ship was still afloat and he put a third torpedo into her, and she did go down, carrying all left aboard with her.

U-703 stopped for a moment to give supplies and directions to the men on the rafts, and then sped off, hunting again.

During all this time the *Tirpitz* and other German capital ships had come out—hesitantly—but then almost immediately had gone back into safety as the Germans realized that the allies were using PQ 17 as bait to get their main fleet units. The convoy had split into sections by the morning of July 6 and had to brave the twin dangers of air attack and submarine attack. Early on the morning of July 6, the freighter *John Witherspoon* began a long engagement with submarine *U-255*, whose captain was *Korvettenkapitaen* Reinhard Reche. The submarine chased the merchant ship, and the merchant ship's gun crew fired at the submarine every time the wake of the periscope could be seen. Finally, at 4:40 in the afternoon, Reche fired a spread of four torpedoes at the merchantman; a pillar of smoke and fire jumped up 200 feet in the air and settled.

But not quickly enough. Reche came up closer and gave her another torpedo, which caused the *John Witherspoon* to break in half and slowly fall back beneath the sea.

Planes and U-Boats competed now for targets. A JU 88 came up near the entrance to the White Sea and bombed the *Pan Atlantic*, sinking her just under the noses of *U-88* and *U-703*, which had been stalking the ship for hours.

The slaughter went on. And while U-Boats were going back to base, leaving only six in the area, another three: *U-251*, *U-376*, and *U-408* were just about to be dispatched with full tanks of fuel and loaded torpedo racks.

On the sixth day of July the German high command was convinced that all but six or seven of the ships of PQ 17 had been sunk, and they behaved accordingly. If fact more than half the convoy was still at sea, hiding from the enemy or dispersed.

But German propaganda was well served because when the big German ships threatened to come out and the British scattered the convoy and took away most of the escorts, it appeared to the Germans that the whole convoy had broken up in panic.

Many of the remaining ships of the convoy moved to a harbor in Novaya Zemlya, the new land, which is north of their destination. Other ships tried to make Archangel or Murmansk on their own. And the U-Boats were still in pursuit. *Fregattenkapitaen* Reche in *U-255* chased the *Alcoa Ranger*, an American freighter, and sank her. Headquarters ordered him and four other U-Boat commanders to form a patrol line across Matochkin Strait, but many ships had already slipped through by July 7. One, however, did not escape the net here, and it was sighted just before three o'clock in the afternoon by *Korvetten-*

kapitaen Guenther LaBaume in *U-355*. The ship
was the *Hartlebury,* and as it turned out, she was
the 21st ship of this big convoy to fall to the
Germans. LaBaume took careful aim from the
short distance of 800 yards and fired all four of
his forward torpedo tubes at her. The torpedoes
snaked out, and 12 feet below the surface they
ran swiftly and straight toward the merchantman. The seconds went by, 10, 20, 30—47 seconds—
and then the explosions came and threw a curtain of smoke and spray over the ship so that
from LaBaume's periscope the whole ship was
blotted out.

Aboard the *Hartlebury,* the third officer had
just relieved the second mate who was going
down to the cabin for tea, and the third mate was
walking on the bridge when the first torpedo
exploded and threw a shower of debris and a
curtain of water right across the bridge. He was
hit on the head and knocked down. The first
officer was knocked down and his arm broken.
The radio officer was knocked out, and the radio
was destroyed. There would be no SOS reports
from *Hartlebury.*

The captain was trapped under a wing of the
bridge which had collapsed, but the first officer
managed to free him, and they surveyed the damage. The ship was listing. The engines had
stopped, and the boilers were blowing steam. The
ship carried two lifeboats but one of them had
been crushed, and the crew pushed to the other,
while the captain and first officer went astern
and released life rafts. Then a terrible thing happened: the young cadet who had been told to
lower the falls on the remaining lifeboat let go
the forward one, and the nose of the boat crashed
into the sea. A dozen men had disobeyed orders
in their panic and jumped into the boat while it

was still in the davits, and now they were spilled
into the freezing water as the boat filled up.

The ship had two jollyboats and the cooks and
firemen got one of them out and lowered it, with
three men in it. But they had forgotten to put
the plugs in the bottom—and the boat sank, taking them to their deaths. A man could not long
survive even in the summer in the icy waters of
northern Russia.

The ship was settling as the first officer got
the life raft into the water, and although the raft
was designed for eight men, there were 13 aboard
it. But after two rafts were launched, both full,
there were still some 20 men and the second and
third officers aboard the ship, without a boat,
without rafts. Their only hope lay in the flooded
lifeboat that was still being towed along, half
sunk by its after fall. Many of them slid down
ropes and got into this boat and tried to free it.

Aboard the U-Boat, Captain LaBaume was not
very happy with the way the *Hartlebury* continued to float, and he turned the boat around and
fired his stern tube from 1000 yards. The torpedo
hit, broke the ship's back, and she took a violent
list to port.

Men were still climbing into the lifeboat. The
second officer was clambering down hand over
hand when a steward seized an axe and cut the
single rope that still kept the boat tied to the
ship. The lifeboat fell into the sea, half swamped,
and the second officer was left hanging in the
air.

In the boat, some 20 men bailed furiously just
as the ship broke into three parts and began to
sink. As the stern section raised high in the air,
the captain jumped into the water and landed
next to the half-swamped boat. The third officer
picked him up.

As they moved away from the ship, they saw

the second officer, still aboard, and as they watched he stripped off his life jacket, his coat, and his cap and waved to them. He had given up hope of rescue and was prepared to die with the ship.

As the *Hartlebury* went down, *U-355* cruised slowly up to the lifeboat on the surface, and the crew emerged to man the guns, which they trained on the men in the boats. Captain LaBaume then asked for Captain Stephenson of the *Hartlebury* and the details of this ship. The captain was silent. LaBaume then gave the men on one of the rafts a bottle of gin and a bottle of rum and some food and directions to the nearest land, knowing full well their chances of making it were very dim. LaBaume and his men could have helped— they could at least have freed the half-swamped boat of its burden of water. But they were not helpful. *U-355* sped away, leaving the men to their fate.

That fate was much the same as the end of most of those who had to take to the boats in this Arctic climate, even though in this case they were only three miles from land.

The men began to die. They lay back and grew very sleepy and dropped off. Able Seaman Geoffrey Dixon began talking strangely about an hour after the U-Boat left them, and then raved, and, sitting up to his armpits in water, began ducking his head to try to drown himself. Others restrained him, but then he seemed to go to sleep, and then his eyes came open and the third officer knew he was dead. He and another picked up the body and slid it gently into the sea.

In two hours many in the boat were dead, the firemen first of all, because they came up from the engine room in their undershirts. They slipped down and were very quiet and then they died.

The young steward who had cut the rope that

freed the lifeboat volunteered to swim to a life raft which seemed more apt to survive than the boat, and he tried, but foundered, and they hauled him back in the boat. His feet then began to freeze.

The cruel fate of many was the salvation of the few; as the men died and were pushed overboard, the boat began to lighten, and by morning, when there were only five of the original 20 left alive in the boat, it had stopped shipping water, and they had a chance of survival.

But not much of a chance. They tried to get the mast up but were not strong enough to step it completely. They raised the sail, but it hung at a crazy angle and did not draw the wind. One of the men lost heart and jumped over the side. He swam away into the fog that surrounded them and disappeared.

Aboard the big raft there were 14 men where nine were supposed to ride, and the last four had to stand up. Standing saved their lives—they were the only four to survive the night. The last to die was the second engineer, who kept repeating the Twenty-Third Psalm over and over again as he weakened.

"The Lord is my shepherd

"I shall not want . . ."

It died away into a mumble, and he was gone.

In the morning a small raft drifted up and one living man transferred to the big raft. These men drifted for two more days and then, when the fog lifted, found they were less than a mile from shore and were rescued by the boat of an American ship that was beached there on the coast.

On the one raft that had been given food and drink, all nine survived, passing the bottles around and massaging their limbs to prevent frostbite. They found the captain and the half-sunk lifeboat and rescued them too, made their way to a little island, and finally joined the others near the beached American ship. Twenty men of the crew of 56 survived.

And at sea, still the U-Boats hunted. Seven of them remained in the area on the night of July 7, cruising around the coast of Novaya Zemlya, searching. Reche in *U-255* torpedoed the *Olopana*, a Matson steamer, and then surfaced and sank her with his guns as the crew escaped on rafts. He wanted to sink her quickly so other ships would not be warned that he was there, but then he learned that the radio operator of *Olopana* had gotten off a distress signal, so he sped away, looking elsewhere and leaving the men struggling for the slender hold they had on life aboard those rafts.

Next night, July 8, Admiral Schmundt decided that the operation against convoy PQ 17 had come nearly to an end. *U-88* was moving home, short of fuel, and six boats remained in the area. He ordered them to make one last sweep and then to come home. They searched, and meanwhile a little convoy of four merchant ships and a dozen escorts moved toward the White Sea and safety. *U-703, U-375,* and *U-408* found this convoy and tried to attack, but there were too many escorts—and they were depth charged. One submarine fired two torpedoes, but they missed. Still, they got the word to Norway that the convoy, or part of it, was still moving, and the bombers came again. They so damaged the merchantman *Hoosier* that a corvette had to sink it. There was more bombing, more damage, but the U-Boats' work was finished.

In the end, bombers and submarines had accounted for 22 of the 35 merchant ships that set sail for Russia in PQ 17, and a rescue ship and a fleet oiler had also been sunk. The total was 142,000 tons of shipping lost in this one operation, and in terms of the war that meant 3350 trucks and cars, 430 tanks, 210 bombers in crates, and 99,000 tons of supplies such as radar sets, food, and ammunition. It was enough to equip an army.

The German U-Boats and bombers had done their job.

CHAPTER SIX

In the Balance

The trouble with the diversion of so many U-Boats to Norwegian and Arctic waters was that it cut down the number of submarines available to Admiral Doenitz for the major effort, the war in the Atlantic. Doenitz knew from the beginning and always maintained that the Atlantic war was the key to the whole German effort, once Fortress Europe had been established. He recognized that the tremendous economic power of the United States would be thrown against Germany on the side of Britain and that the material for invasion of Europe would come across the Atlantic. Therefore he struggled constantly to fight the Atlantic battle.

In those first six months of 1942 when the U-Boats sank nearly 600 ships, by far the largest number were sunk in American waters, with a loss in this area of only half a dozen boats. But this was to change, as the Americans geared up for the war they had been so badly prepared to fight. And because of this lack of preparation and the preoccupation of the American navy with its battle for life in the Pacific, the period of October 1942 to the spring of 1943 would go down in naval history as the Bloody Winter.

By the autumn of 1942 the Americans were using the convoy system, but it was a mark of the German position at that moment that Doenitz was, in effect, reading the American mail, as on October 20, 1942, when the U.S. navy sent a secret radio message to the British authorities, announcing the plans for convoy SC 107. The British got the message. So did the Germans, whose cryptographic service deciphered the message and had it in Admiral Doenitz' hands in his Paris headquarters as soon as the British had it in London. So when the 22 ships of the convoy sailed on October 24 from the New York harbor, the Germans knew and were ready.

SC 107 set out for sea, escorted by a destroyer, a corvette, and a minesweeper. Six days later, having flushed one submarine on the surface, the convoy moved to a prearranged point near Cape Race, where it picked up 20 more ships and changed over to the mid-ocean escort. That changeover was something relatively new—representing the new strength of the combined American and British forces. No longer did convoys go anywhere unescorted. But the odds were still heavy for the Germans, because SC 107 was to have only the destroyer HMS *Restigouche* and four small corvettes, which could not travel any faster on the surface than a fast Altantic U-Boat. And ahead of them, waiting, were 15 U-Boats stretched out in a north-south line across the convoy lane. The deciphered message had told where the convoy was coming and approximately when.

Kapitaenleutnant Herbert Schneider in *U-522* was the first to spot the convoy. He was cruising on the surface south of Cape Race on October 30 when a lookout shouted. He had seen smoke on the starboard bow. In a moment Schneider was on the bridge, and he looked and then ordered.

The boat turned toward the smoke, picked up speed, and raced across the surface until he identified a corvette and the masts of several ships. There was the convoy.

The alarm sounded, and the officer and four lookouts of the watch scurried for the hatch. The captain came last, as the siren sounded throughout the boat, and the submarine began to slide down into the sea.

Through his periscope, Captain Schneider began to watch the convoy. He identified it as a group of 14 ships (for that is all he saw). And for an hour he moved along watching, checking to get the mean course of the zigzagging convoy. He wrote out a message for headquarters and sent it. Back on the surface, he waited for Doenitz to answer. The reply was not long in coming. It ordered all the other U-Boats of this pack, called Group Violet, to come to the position announced by *U-522*. Schneider was to track the convoy and report every two hours. So night came, and the pack gathered as the convoy steamed along, making perhaps an average of seven knots.

The radio operator of the destroyer *Restigouche* picked up strong U-Boat signals, and from shore now came a radio fix on the transmission, showing its position. The destroyer captain could assume that the U-Boat had found them. He broke radio silence and asked for air cover.

The air cover was already arriving, in a sense, from the Royal Canadian Air Force. A plane had found *U-520*, one of the pack, and had bombed and sunk it. Another airplane was now in the process of finding *U-658* and would sink that submarine, too. Then the enemy of the convoys closed in—the weather turned foul. All flights were cancelled. At least there was one bright spot, as the radio men picked up the tweetering of the U-Boats as they moved in: from the original escort group the destroyer *Walker* had remained temporarily with the convoy. She was the same ship that had dealt with Captains Kretschmer and Schepke, and although she had a new captain, she had plenty of experience in just this work. She would be needed, too, for within a few hours the convoy would come to the Greenland Air Gap, that area in mid-Atlantic where no aircraft could cover the ships at sea. The U-Boats had learned not to concentrate here, in what they called the Devil's Gorge. For three days the convoy would be on its own.

For SC 107 the action began that Sunday afternoon, November 1, when *U-438,* which was now assigned to contact the convoy, noted that one of the ships was straggling. She worked her way around in front of the straggling ship, dived, and from periscope depth sent one torpedo. But it was a long shot, and it missed. It missed so far that not even the straggling ship was aware that an attempt had just been made on its life.

The margin of safety of the convoy was cut a little that day when *Walker* had to turn around and go back to the Canadian coast for other duty. Only one destroyer now, instead of the two. And the one, *Restigouche,* was just waiting for the attack its captain knew would come. Lt. Comdr. Desmond N. Piers, that captain, had been warned by radio and was being warned again.

The Nazi plan was to concentrate the wolf pack around the convoy and then, when the convoy entered the area where air coverage was absent, to go to work. The two U-Boats which had been lost had been too far to the west, but soon the safety zone for U-Boats and murder zone for ships would be reached.

By sunset the concentration of U-Boats around the convoy was intense and the escorts knew it. The highly developed direction-finding equipment at sea and ashore told Captain Piers that one U-Boat was only eight miles away, on the port of the convoy. He sent the corvette *Celandine* after the submarine.

There were eight U-Boats around the convoy now and only five escorts. It was obvious that something was going to happen. Toward nightfall, *Restigouche* went after a submarine that was trailing the convoy and chased, depth charging. But while she was so occupied, *Kapitaenleutnant* Baron Siegfried von Forstner in *U-402* slipped between the destroyer and the convoy, came up quickly on the surface past the corvette *Arvida* (whose radar was out of order), and soon was right in the convoy, 800 yards from a ship. Still on the surface, von Forstner used the bridge attack sight, which was a telescope connected to the torpedo attack computer, brought a freighter into the cross hairs, and set up the firing information in the computer that controlled the torpedoes. His first torpedo misfired, and so did the second, which ran erratically. They were so close now that the column of fire and debris came back down around them and the concussion shook up the deck crew of the submarine. He had hit the ship *Empire Sunrise,* and she would float for two hours while the crew fought and then finally abandoned ship, picked up by a rescue ship. But right now von Forstner had no time to concern himself with this ship. An escort had come running to the scene, and he had to take action and save himself.

"Alarm" came the cry, and the siren sounded loud through the U-Boat. Von Forstner and his deck crew hastened into the conning tower and he dogged the hatch behind him as the water surged up around it. Less than two minutes from the second that the lookout had spotted the escort, the submarine was at 300 feet. The depth charging began, but it was not even close. He moved back to just under 200 feet and kept the boat there, staying down for several hours but sticking with the convoy.

Around midnight, another submarine very nearly torpedoed the destroyer *Restigouche*. *U-381* got the destroyer in the sights, but Piers was a canny captain, and even when he did not see trouble, he behaved as though it were around him. He was zigzagging as he patrolled, and as he zigged, *U-381* fired four torpedoes at him from periscope depth. But then *Restigouche* zagged, and all the torpedoes missed by so wide a margin that the destroyer did not even know she had been attacked.

Just after this event, von Forstner surfaced again and fired a spread of five torpedoes from 1000 yards, aiming at several ships. One torpedo hit *Rinos* and another *Dalcroy,* both in the port column. The former ship sank very quickly, the other was set afire. And now many other events occurred, one after the other, as the U-Boats attacked in force. *U-84* fired two torpedoes at a freighter but missed with both. *U-522* fired four torpedoes and hit the ship *Hartington* with two of them. She sank in 15 minutes. Two things had become apparent now: that the new breed of submarine commanders was not of the calibre of the Priens and Kretschmers, but that what they lacked in experience and ability was made up for by sheer numbers. There was plenty of missing. *U-438* stood out and fired a torpedo from long range and missed. *U-521* fired from outside and missed with three torpedoes. But for these inadequacies there was a von Forstner, who came in now on the surface and sank *Empire Leopard,* only standing out 1400 yards from the port column to fire the deadly spread of four torpedoes. He was so aggressive that he came in too close and took a hit in the conning tower from a three-inch gun on a merchant ship. But he evened that score quickly enough by sinking *Empire Leopard* and then *Empire Antelope,* another merchantman.

On the other side of the convoy, Herbert Schneider in *U-522* was also creating his share of havoc. He fired a spread of five torpedoes from the surface and hit the steamer *Maritima.* Just before he fired the area had been lit up by star shells from the corvettes. After his torpedoes struck *Maritima* there was no need to fire any more star shells for a while, for that ship was carrying munitions, and she exploded with a roar that shook the whole neighborhood. Five other merchantmen around her were shaken so badly by the concussion that they reported they were torpedoed and turned on their lights. One of the ships stopped its engines, its engineer thinking it was sinking. The captain of another ordered the ship abandoned. The *Maritima* blew itself apart now and sank in three minutes, and 32 members of the crew were never seen again.

Schneider was impressed with that explosion, but he was very busy, too. A few minutes later, he fired more torpedoes and sank *Mount Pelion.* Then moved off, for it was growing late; dawn was near and the time for the submarines to submerge and track the convoy had come again. From way outside, *U-521* and *U-442* fired a few torpedoes, but they ran through the convoy, not hitting anything. Then the struggle ended for the day.

They were in no hurry. Another night would come, with the convoy still in the Devil's Gorge, and there would be more opportunity. Several of the U-Boats now converged and awaited the coming of a tanker U-Boat to refuel them. The others stood off—all but Captain Schneider in *U-522.* He surfaced at dawn, sent a report to Doenitz about his sinkings (claiming seven ships which was a gross exaggeration), and then raced ahead of the convoy to make a daylight attack. He let the convoy come to him, and at periscope depth torpedoed the *Parthenon,* then dived quickly.

Above, the corvette *Arvida* and destroyer *Restigouche* came after the U-Boat and dropped several patterns of depth charges. But it was the mark of the new Atlantic boats that they could go deep and stay deep, and Schneider was down to around 500 feet. *Arivida* made a contact and shook up the U-Boat badly with depth charges, but not badly enough to put her out of action. Schneider wanted revenge, too, and as darkness came down he found the convoy, and this time fired at an escort, but he missed.

In a way, this second night found weather on the side of the convoy, for it was very filthy, and as the dark closed in so did the fog, which sheltered the ships, but also made many of them miss the convoy commander's signals. Hearing of the plight of this convoy, the powers that were on the other side of the Atlantic detached a destroyer and a corvette from other work and added them to the protective force of SC 107 and they were on tap this night. The U-Boats stayed away, keeping track but not trying to attack. Shooting from outside was almost hopeless, and to go in among the ships in the fog meant to run the very grave danger of being cut down by a merchantman. So the U-Boats waited.

At dawn the impatient U-Boats began to act again. *U-438* fired two torpedoes from outside and missed. *U-521* fired and hit the tanker *Hahira.* She flamed up and a few of the crew escaped her, then the fire went out. She dropped back, and *Restigouche* went back with her. Captain Piers was trying to protect the ship, although how long he could do so was doubtful. He made a contact with a submarine (it was *U-522*) and depth charged, without hurting the U-Boat. But that was the trouble from the convoy point of view, and the beauty of it from the U-Boat point of view. Even as *Restigouche* was occupying herself with *U-522*, not far away *U-521* came up on the other side of *Hahira* and put another torpedo into her from 800 yards, and still another one, even though a corvette came rushing up to help. The third torpedo sank that tanker.

So night came again, and with it a new threat. The U-Boats had been in touch with Paris headquarters all day long and reported that the convoy was still big and still moving. Admiral Doenitz then decided to commit a new wolf pack to the convoy, Group Natter, which consisted of 15 more U-Boats, all of them well fueled and carrying full torpedoes.

In Liverpool, where Admiral Sir Percy Noble held forth as commander of the Western Approaches, the staff recognized that the convoy was in terrible danger, and this same night detached three more ships, an American coast guard cutter and two destroyers, the *Schenck* and the *Leary*, to rush to the aid of SC 107.

So night fell on November 3, with aid coming to both sides and the U-Boats and the convoy locked in battle.

Kapitaenleutnant Dietrich Lohmann in *U-89* started off the action this night, moving into the convoy itself in the manner of Kretschmer of old, aided this night by the flicker of the northern lights and good visibility. But even visibility would not have granted Doenitz the boon that fate now gave. *U-89* chose for her torpedoes the *Jeypore*, which was the ship of the convoy commander. *U-89* fired two more torpedoes, missed another ship, and then sped out of the convoy, as the phosphate cargo of *Jeypore* began to burn. Everyone aboard the merchantman knew that beneath the phosphate was a load of munitions, so no time was wasted in abandoning ship.

And now the wolf pack got down to work, taking advantage of the conditions that favored them so greatly. *U-132* torpedoed the *Hobbema*, then moved over and hit *Empire Lynx* and *Hatimura*, knocking both ships out of the convoy. *Empire Lynx* blew up, but the big explosion of the night came just afterward, from one of the torpedoed ships. It was so severe that all the ships around were shaken, submarines were jolted, and *U-132* disappeared. No one saw her go, no escort reported a sinking, but *U-132* just never showed up again. She had apparently been too close in the convoy when the *Hobbema* blew up.

The big explosion shook everyone and put an end to the night's sinkings. Then came many changes, showing how oddly the sea war could surge back and forth. By morning, the weather had worsened and the wolf pack had lost contact with the convoy. Most of the U-Boats were low on fuel and torpedoes now anyhow. The new wolf pack, coming up, was diverted by Doenitz to a westbound convoy discovered on the way to the scene. The last attack on the convoy was made on the night of November 4, by *U-89,* which came in and sank the freighter *Daleby*. She hung around the fringes, prepared to attack again, but time was running out. By morning the convoy had reached the end of the Devil's Gorge, and *U-89* was to learn that with a shock. In the morning, she was moving along the surface, when suddenly out of nowhere came a B-24 bomber, which straddled with depth charges. The charges blew and sent *U-89* reeling. She managed to escape—just barely—and limped back to Lorient for repairs.

The B-24 responded now to the radio direction

of the destroyer *Restigouche*, which had fixes on several members of the wolf pack, not far from the convoy. The plane made two more attacks and drove two more submarines down deep. They came up, later, to report to Doenitz that the air cover was intensive, and he told them to refrain from attacking until the next day, and then he called off the U-Boats completely, for the area was too dangerous for them. Times had changed.

So SC 107, or what was left of it, now moved safely on to its destination. In the beginning the convoy had been safe, and two U-Boats had been sunk. Then had come the terrible three days of sailing in the open sea, without air cover, and 15 ships had been sunk. Then, as soon as air cover was available again, the situation changed. It was apparent that the balance in the Atlantic was changing too. What was not quite so apparent was that the attitude of both sides in this war was becoming hardened. U-Boats were now doing nothing to save or help the survivors of the ships they sank. And the hunter-killer groups of the allies regarded the U-Boats as enemies more deadly and dastardly than cobras. This autumn, a few weeks before the sailing of SC 107, had come an event that was to play an epochal role in the use of U-Boats and in the war against them.

It had begun in September in the warm seas off Africa, and the first group of characters in the drama were Captain Werner Hartenstein and the crew of the *U-156*, an Atlantic U-Boat built in 1941.

On the morning of September 12, *U-156* was cruising on the surface of the Atlantic, five degrees south of the equator, when a lookout shouted that he saw a smoke cloud. Hartenstein ordered the boat full ahead on both diesels, which meant he was making 16 knots. As he chased the smoke cloud grew larger. An hour and a half went by, but the captain of the U-Boat now saw that it would be a long chase, because the other ship was moving almost as fast as he was. By one o'clock in the afternoon Hartenstein could make out the lines of the ship through his binoculars. She was a liner, either an auxiliary cruiser or a troopship now, and Hartenstein was already counting his chickens. Her sinking would bring his submarine's tonnage up to 100,000. But that sinking would have to wait until darkness.

By six o'clock that evening, the captain of the submarine had decided that his quarry was, indeed, a merchant cruiser. Two hours later Hartenstein had worked himself into an approach position and dived to make his attack. Just after eight o'clock, in the darkness, he took careful aim, using the computer machinery, and sent his tin fish from tubes one and three toward the ship.

The quarry was in fact the 20,000-ton liner *Laconia* of the Cunard White Star Line, 600 feet long, carrying a full complement of passengers and prisoners of war from the campaign against the Italians in Libya. They had sailed from Suez, around the Horn, and were heading they knew not quite where, because their sailing orders had been changed just a few hours before. Originally, the ship was scheduled to go into Freetown on the West African coast, but she had been put on a new course by the Admiralty. She was carrying more than 2700 people—460 of the crew, military passengers, civilians, and 1800 Italian prisoners of war.

Just after eight o'clock, the first torpedo struck *Laconia* on the starboard side, and then the second, even as the ship began to list. In the confusion, prisoners, soldiers, sailors, and the crew and passengers milled about to get into the lifeboats. Some panicked. Lifeboats went over the sides half empty. And there were moments of heroism as officers gave women and children their life jackets and crewmen worked to save the passengers. In Number 4 hold, where the first torpedo had struck, there had been 450 Italian prisoners, and most of these were killed. The second torpedo hit at Number 2 hold, where there were also Italian prisoners.

Aboard the submarine, the officers and men were congratulating themselves, for they thought they had torpedoed a troop ship and sent a regimen of men to the bottom. Then they heard the distress transmission of the *Laconia*. It was an SSS message—which meant *Laconia* was warning the world that she had been torpedoed and that the submarine which did it was in the area. When Captain Hartenstein heard the message, he was furious and decided to go back and capture the captain of the ship. For half an hour the wireless operators sent out their message telling of the attack and warning ships behind, by giving the position and the time of attack. The boats continued to leave the ship, and some men trusted themselves to the life rafts on deck. One boat went into the water with its plug out, but the passengers discovered the problem in time and stuffed the hole with cloth. Some were trapped in the ship, some were attacked by barracuda and killed there in the water as they fled the sinking ship, which was going down by the bows. And down she went, just before 9:30. Moving toward his prey, Captain Hartenstein did not know that he was cheated of his chance to capture who had offended him. The *Laconia's* master, Captain Rudolph Sharp, had chosen to go down with his ship in the old tradition.

As the submarine approached, Hartenstein saw that *Laconia* had not sunk, and then he saw the people struggling in boats, on rafts, and in the water. He watched the ship, her stern high out of the water, and he passed close by several boats but ignored them and the people in them.

Then he and his officers heard the cries.

"Aiuto!"

"That's Italian," said one of his men. And they looked at each other. They moved by two swimmers and stopped, then pulled them aboard and discovered that they were Italians and prisoners of war. Hartenstein did not speak Italian, but soon he figured out that there were some 1000 POWs on the ship he had sunk—prisoners who were allies of the Third Reich. He began hauling out more prisoners and finally found one Italian who spoke enough German to give the submarine captain enough of the story of *Laconia* so that Hartenstein was worried. He knew now that there were also women and children on the boat.

What was to be done? The *Laconia* had transmitted her warning message until the power on the ship went out, and so many times that the U-Boat captain was certain the SSS had been picked up by enemy warships. If so, they would be coming this way. According to the laws Hitler had promulgated, he had no responsibility except to save his submarine. Yet these Italians were allies. He thought hard and then made his decision. He would begin rescue operations. Soon the submarine had 90 people aboard, besides the crew, and was jammed everywhere but in the control room and conning tower, which the captain had ordered kept free.

That night many struggled in the water or in the boats and rafts for survival, and many died. And while the drama was played in this little section of the sea, at U-Boat headquarters in Paris, Admiral Doenitz was learning from Hartenstein's messages a little of what had happened.

He had been awakened, a procedure he was used to and on which he insisted. *Korvettenkapitaen* Guenther Hessler, his chief of operations (and his son-in-law), informed him that 1500 Italians had been sunk in a British ship. Doenitz, assaying the political implications as far as Italy was concerned, decided that the rescue attempt must be continued and furthered. He examined his big U-Boat chart on the wall, found three U-Boats that might manage to get into the area in time, and ordered them to head for the position reported by *U-156*.

One of these boats was *U-507* commanded by *Korvettenkapitaen* Harro Schacht, which had been working off the coasts of North and South America. He was two days away. Second was *U-506*, commanded by *Kapitaenleutnant* Wuerdemann, which was a little closer. Third was *U-459*, a tanker submarine commanded by *Leutnant* von Wilamowitz-Moellendorf, and he did not even make an attempt to go to the rescue, because he decided he was too far away from the scene.

Morning came on Sunday, September 13, and in their little spheres of woe, the survivors of *Laconia* waited. They did not know it, but when the ship had gone down, taking her captain, she had also taken about a thousand of the others, killed outright, wounded, trapped, or just too confused to escape the sinking ship. The water was warm at least, but it also had stinging jellyfish, which harried the survivors. And then there was the sun. During the day, the survivors in the boats looked for those in the sea, and by nightfall all those left alive in the water had been moved to boats. And Captain Hartenstein had been picking up more men. On the second day he had 193 survivors aboard the submarine.

Messages flowed back and forth between the submarine and Paris headquarters. Hartenstein suggested that the area be "neutralized" and that other ships of all nations be invited to come and help with the rescue, promising of course to leave the submarine alone. Doenitz was in touch with Grand Admiral Raeder, and soon the Italians were informed and dispatched the submarine *Capellini* to assist. They headed for the area, where some 16 or 18 lifeboats (nobody was quite sure) floated in the sea.

Hartenstein was worried about his submarine and checked often on her trim. He sent a message in English in the clear, promising that if any ship would come to help he would not attack, as long as he was not attacked by ships or planes. And he gave his position.

In Paris, when this message was picked up, Doenitz' staff was very critical of Hartenstein. They felt sure he was first asking to be attacked by the enemy. Their position was enhanced when Hitler himself warned that the safety of the U-Boat and U-Boat operations must not be endangered by this rescue attempt. Hitler said the French ought to send ships from Dakar to rescue the survivors. Operations Chief Hessler wanted to break off the rescue operations and send Hartenstein to safety. Doenitz would not agree. He told Hartenstein to stay in the area but to be alert and ready to submerge at once. Lt. Comdr. Marco Revedin, the captain of *Capellini*, was at this time heading as quickly as he could go for the area. In Dakar, the French admiral was just dispatching the French sloop of war *Dumond'Urville* to the area, but her captain knew as he set out that he could not reach the place before the evening of September 16. Other French ships also began to move, including a cruiser, the *Gloire*.

Onboard *U-156*, Captain Hartenstein and his crew were treating the survivors, including several women, as well as humanly possible. They

were fed the same food as the U-Boat crew and
given water and even sunburn cream and other
medicines. By Monday morning, Hartenstein sent
a message to Paris saying he had 200 survivors
on rafts and in lifeboats, and another 200 on his
submarine. But the heat and the exposure and
the sea were taking their toll and men and women
were dying. Some boats had already set out for
the coast of Africa. Some floated around the area
still.

Hartenstein waited. On the morning of September 15, Wuerdemann arrived in *U-506* and
took 132 of the 260 unwilling passengers who
had now crowded aboard the U-Boat. That done,
the two submarines began cruising toward the
sunken wreck, looking for more survivors. Hartenstein kept the boats around him and moved people from boats to submarine for treatment and
rest, and then back in the boats again. He could
not possibly accommodate all these people on the
submarine permanently. Some boats were sent
on their way, with food and water, toward shore.

U-506 cruised and rescued more survivors until she had more than 200 people on board and
was giving out quantities of fresh water and food
to people in boats. Then up came Captain Schacht
in *U-507*, to take aboard another 153 survivors.
The boats now had three protectors, and the people a fair chance for survival.

In Paris and Berlin the rescue operation was
bringing a good deal of pressure on Doenitz and
his command. Hitler was not very pleased about
it and warned Doenitz not to endanger a submarine, this for the second time. But it seemed that
the submarines would be relieved by the French
ships soon. On the morning of September 16,
Captain Hartenstein had such a message from
the Doenitz headquarters. Then, at 11:25, a four-
engined plane flew over the submarine, a B-24

bomber, then flew away. The Germans unfurled a red-cross flag, but the bomber paid no attention, came in, and dropped several bombs, blowing up one lifeboat and damaging the submarine. Hartenstein did not shoot back, but when he found that his U-Boat was threatened he regretted it. He was going to have to submerge and he might have to fight, in spite of the spirit that had prompted this rescue mission. He ordered the British off the boat, and both men and women came up and jumped into the sea. Then, he discovered that the batteries had gotten wet and were beginning to give off chlorine gas. He would have to evacuate the Italians, too. So he did, and soon there was no one left on *U-156* except the crew. The submarine crew got to work to repair damage and did repair it.

But now Hartenstein had had enough. If the Americans or British or whoever it was were going to bomb the survivors and kill them, then he was going to abandon the rescue. And he did. He sent a message to Doenitz announcing that he was abandoning rescue operations, and he sailed westward. He would have to return to France and a U-Boat base to get his boat entirely seaworthy once again.

At the Paris headquarters, the U-Boat commanding staff was furious to learn of the betrayal of the rescue by what was actually an American plane responding to British instructions to attack. Captain Eberhard Godt, the chief of staff, and Hessler wanted Doenitz to break off the rescue attempt entirely and abandon all the survivors of *Laconia*. But Doenitz would not. He ordered *U-506* and *U-507* to wait for the French ships to arrive, hand over the survivors, and then leave—but also to watch out for attack and dive any time, if one seemed to threaten. He also ordered the submarines to put all but the Italians in the boats.

But while Doenitz did this, he also gave long and comprehensive thought to the whole problem of submarines, rescues, and air attacks. The airplane was changing the submarine war more than anyone had expected. So he drafted an order to his commanders covering their future conduct in terms of rescues and the safety of their submarines. He put it aside for the moment, however.

Around noon on the fifth day of the operation, *U-506* was attacked, too, by another plane, but she dived and was unhurt. The rescue operation continued. On the morning of September 17, the cruiser *Gloire* approached the area and rescued the first boatload of survivors and in the afternoon came upon *U-507*, which was loaded with Italians. She and *Annamite*, another French ship, began taking the survivors aboard, while *U-506* submerged and kept watch to guarantee the safety of her sister U-Boat. Then *U-506* transshipped her survivors, and the two French ships moved off to look for other boats, and then the submarines submerged and left the area. The Italian submarine had also picked up some survivors and turned them over to the French, so that in the end 1091 of the 2700 people who had been aboard *Laconia* were saved. And then Doenitz issued his famous *Laconia* order:

No attempt was to be made to rescue the crews of ships the U-Boats sank. No one was to be picked up out of the water and put into lifeboats; no capsized lifeboats were to be turned over or bailed out. No food or water was to be given out to survivors. In other words, the whole idea of rescue was to be abandoned and outlawed by the Germans as counter to the primary demands of the war for destruction of enemy ships and their crews. The U-Boats were to be primarily concerned for their own safety.

As for previous instructions, captains of merchant ships and chief engineers were still to be brought in if possible, for their Intelligence value, but other crew members were to be rescued only if they had some Intelligence value. And as for the rest, the U-Boat captains were now to be harsh. The warfare was to be unrestricted. There would be no more quarter given the enemy.

CHAPTER SEVEN

Hell at Sea

The *Laconia* affair had another effect on U-Boat warfare. It was partly responsible for a complete review of the submarine warfare program in the fall of 1942. Doenitz saw the handwriting on the wall. He had already begun work for development of new high-speed submarines powered by Walter hydrogen peroxide turbines, which could remain submerged almost indefinitely. From Dutch designs he had adopted the snorkel or breathing apparatus that let a submarine move underwater using its diesel engines. He was thinking ahead.

At the meetings, Doenitz warned that allied air power would grow ever stronger and possibly would put an end to attacks on the surface. The whole U-Boat war might change drastically, he said, and certainly it was going to grow ever more dangerous. He would need more and newer boats to proceed. Admiral Raeder did not much care for Doenitz' presentation of the sea war. Hitler scoffed at Doenitz' warning that allied air power could really threaten the U-Boat war in the Atlantic. And when the meetings were over, Admiral Raeder acted to limit Doenitz' power to matters of operations alone. Doenitz refused to accept this limitation, and threatened to resign. Meanwhile, Raeder quarreled with Hitler over the use of the pocket battleships and the cruisers, for Hitler had quite lost confidence in this arm of the navy. And as a result, at the end of January, 1943, instead of being retired as he had expected, Doenitz found himself commander in chief of the German navy, while Raeder retired for all practical purposes. The change did not seriously affect day-to-day operations of the U-Boat force, for Doenitz kept personal control of that force. After all, given Hitler's attitude toward the surface ships, the U-Boats *were* the German navy. *Kapitaen* Godt and the staff came to Berlin and set up operational headquarters there.

So the war took on a new, more aggressive aspect in the early months of 1943, as Doenitz got more U-Boats and turned some of his remarkable energy to counteracting the allied antisubmarine warfare developments. He had been helped considerably by Admiral Darlan of the French navy, who gave him secrets the British had given the French earlier about Asdic devices, and by the French *Metox,* which was a device that enabled U-Boat commanders to discover when an enemy was tracking them. The U-Boats were given extra platforms on the conning towers, and these were mounted with twin anti-aircraft guns.

January, 1943, was a particularly wicked month in the Atlantic weather scheme. Convoys were delayed and the U-Boats were kept almost immobilized by storms. One U-Boat group of wolves was stationed on the great circle route from North America to the Canary Islands, and on January 7 the eight boats of this pack patrolled a line west of the Canaries, searching for a convoy of tankers that had been reported to be travelling to Gibraltar from the Caribbean. The U-Boats found the convoy, and in four days sank seven of the nine tankers without losing a single U-Boat. This success did much to restore morale and confidence that had been waning since the repercussions of the *Laconia* affair, and it was shortly afterward that Doenitz became chief of the navy.

Then came February.

Doenitz had 100 U-Boats at sea in the Atlantic, and two groups of them were stationed like sentries on a long line that extended down several hundred miles off Newfoundland.

On February 2, *U-456* encountered convoy HX 224 in a storm and made a single attack. This practice was quite out of character for the U-Boat war of the Atlantic in 1943, but the five other boats in the area were hampered by the storm, and HX 224 was a fast convoy, so Doenitz let *U-456* have its way, and *Korvettenkapitaen* Teichert moved in to attack. That day he sank three ships, and from one tanker later another U-Boat, *U-632*, picked up a survivor for Intelligence purposes. On this occasion, Doenitz' instructions really paid off for the Germans: the survivor told about another convoy, SC 118, which was following behind his.

From German Intelligence interception, Doenitz already had information about SC 118, which was scheduled to leave New York for the North Channel, then head to Russia. But with the interception of HX 224 he had expected that the route would be changed. Now he learned that it was not changed, and he acted.

He sent a wolf pack called Pfeil to the area, searching for 44 merchant ships and tankers which were bound for Murmansk, which had been joined by 19 more ships. He did not know that this convoy was heavily guarded with three British destroyers, three British corvettes, a French corvette, and an American Coast Guard cutter. The convoy had gone along very well for several days, and the convoy had actually *passed through* the picket line set up by the wolf pack, when some idiot (the convoy's heartfelt belief) aboard the steamer *Annik* was playing with a projector that fired flares and accidentally triggered it. The result was a display of star shells in the sky above the convoy that lit it up like a Christmas tree. Twenty miles behind them, *U-187* of the wolf pack was moving the other way when an alert lookout saw the display and called the captain. The wolf pack was alerted.

U-187 sent her message off to Doenitz. As she signalled, her signal was intercepted and located by the direction finders aboard a rescue ship in the convoy. So the Germans knew that the convoy was there, and the convoy knew the German U-Boats were there. The battle was about to be joined.

Getting the fix, HMS *Beverly* speeded to 22 knots and headed for the position. Sure enough, less than an hour later her lookouts sighted *U-187* on the surface and closed to around 4000 yards, when the submarine dived. She began to attack and was joined by the destroyer *Vimy,* which made contact and depth charged in three runs. The U-Boat was badly hit by the charges and surfaced near *Beverly.* The crew abandoned ship, for she was about to go down. *Beverly* picked up 40 officers and men, and *Vimy* picked up three. They were very lucky submariners to be alive.

But now 21 more U-Boats were moving to attack the convoy. And attack they did very soon. The escorts ran around in circles, charging from one area where a HF/DF fix had been made to another. They dropped scores of depth charges. One escort tried to ram a U-Boat but the smaller submarine got inside the turning circle and finally managed to dive. The struggle went all that first night, with the result that several U-Boats were damaged and broke off the attack, although none were sunk. But what was equally impressive: the U-Boats lost contact with the convoy because of the severity of the attack by the escorts.

Then the convoy made another drastic error. The commander decided to change course to avoid the U-Boats, but his radio transmitter failed. Some ships got the signal. Some did not. And the convoy then broke up as some ships went one way and others quite a different way. It was a wonder that the U-Boats did not find and destroy at least a part of the convoy—but luck was with the merchantmen again, and they were not found.

On the night of February 5, B-24s began to arrive over the convoy, and they chased and harried the U-Boats which were in the area. Eleven U-Boats sighted planes and dived and lost contact with the convoy that afternoon. *U-465* was attacked and so badly damaged that she headed back to the French coast.

Meanwhile the ship *Polyktor* had broken down and was straggling, trying desperately to catch up. Unfortunately, she caught up with *U-266* instead, and the U-Boat used just one torpedo to send the ship to the bottom. From the U-Boat viewpoint, the battle was beginning.

Soon three U-Boats were in contact with the convoy, just waiting for darkness. *U-267* surfaced then but was driven down by a B-24 Liberator and then at 450 feet was attacked by a destroyer.

The depth charges knocked out the lights and drove the boat down, down, down—to more than 700 feet. Much deeper and the plates would begin to give and then the pressure hull would collapse. Only at this depth, despite constant effort, were they able to blow all ballast and stop the descent. Then what? They could not surface; the danger was too great. They came back up to 400 feet and moved away on one battery-operated engine. The other had been damaged, and they were trailing a telltale stream of oil. But *U-267* was lucky: the destroyer *Vimy* lost contact with her, and she was able to slink away under the surface for hours, and then make her way toward home.

Next, the Free French corvette *Lobelia* found a U-Boat and forced her to dive.

It was essential, one could now, see, for Doenitz to have large packs of wolves around the convoys, because the guardians of the "sheep" were becoming far too effective. Those U-Boats under attack, even if not seriously damaged, were shaken up enough and worried enough to keep them out of action for hours.

But the action against a U-Boat took time and concentration and in the case of this convoy, the port side was bared by the movements of the four escorts after submarines. So *U-262* was able to approach the port side of the convoy unnoticed and actually get between the outside port column and the next one, a tanker on either side. She fired five torpedoes and managed to hit one ship and sink her. Then, the last torpedo gone, the submarine headed back for the French coast. Her crew relaxed, glad in a way to be heading back to safety, and just then the corvette *Lobelia* came across *U-262* and attacked. The U-Boat crash-dived just in time but then had to go through the depth charge attack, so close as to frighten every man. But again by going very deep this submarine escaped.

So far, the fight against SC 118 was very discouraging for Doenitz. He had lost one U-Boat and several had been so badly damaged as to be out of action. Only 11 boats were available for operation in this area. Of course that was many more than Doenitz had available in the whole Atlantic about a year before, but times had changed, and it took many more submarines to get the job of destroying convoys done. Right at the moment the wolf pack had lost contact with the convoy.

Then, at two o'clock on the morning of February 7, *Kapitaenleutnant* von Forstner in *U-402* made contact again and found the starboard side of the convoy uncovered, because the escorts were out chasing contacts astern.

First von Forstner hit a freighter with one torpedo. She sank. She was the *Toward*.

Then he missed with two torpedoes at a tanker. He turned and fired his stern tube. The tanker shuddered with the explosion but did not sink, so he came back and gave her another torpedo. She went down. She was the *R. E. Hopkins*.

Von Forstner dived, and down below his crew struggled and sweated to reload the torpedo tubes.

Meanwhile, the corvettes and destroyers rushed to pay attention to the starboard side of the convoy, and *U-614* slipped in on the port side and torpedoed the freighter *Harmala*.

This torpedoing of three ships in about 20 minutes created a considerable confusion in the convoy. Two escorts rushed to help survivors, and they left only two others to cover the stern of the convoy, and they became involved and then there were none.

Back came von Forstner in the darkness, from the stern, and he torpedoed the tanker *Daghild* which began to sink. It was 0340.

Then, as the corvette *Lobelia* stopped to rescue survivors of *Harmala*, *U-609* came in to investigate and was unlucky to be picked up by the corvette's radar and then by her Asdic. The hunt was on. The submarine dived, and underwater changed course. The corvette changed right with her and moved in ahead and dropped 10 charges. Poor *U-609* ran right into them; there was one particularly loud explosion, a large air bubble broke water, the Asdic pattern faded out and finally disappeared altogether. What was left of *U-609* and her crew sank slowly 12,000 feet to the bottom of the sea.

With their radar and their Asdic and the number of escorts, the convoy protectors were able to carry a very strong war against the U-Boats. Now *Abelia* found a target, another U-Boat on the surface, and rushed up to ram. The U-Boat crash-dived, the corvette depth charged, and the corvette very nearly sank another U-Boat, but she escaped to get away—out of the fight.

Von Forstner now came back in, spotted the freighter *Afrika,* just after 0530, and then attacked the *Henry Mallory,* a freighter-passenger ship that was carrying a number of troops and merchant mariners to Iceland. Of the nearly 500 people aboard, only 175 got into the boats, and a few more got onto rafts. Swimmers tried but died in the icy water. Rescue was a long time in coming in the confusion of the early morning hours.

Then von Forstner moved again, and this time sank the Greek ship *Kalliopi*. He moved off, submerged, loaded his last torpedo into a tube, and then trailed the convoy during the daylight hours like a shark more than a wolf, waiting for stragglers. He surfaced and dived—seven times during the day he was forced to dive, but he kept after the convoy until just after midnight and then used that last torpedo to sink the British ship *Newton Ash*. He wanted to go home then, but Doenitz would not let him. The Admiral ordered von Forstner to shadow the convoy and wait for other U-Boats to come up. Doenitz wanted more ships.

Doenitz still had not learned how dangerous the transmission of continuous signals could be. Von Forstner did as he was told, but the convoy's HF/DF ship got a fix on *U-402,* and they very nearly got von Forstner that night. She headed home with one engine running and much other damage. As dawn came up, bombers based in Ireland moved in over the convoy, which had passed out of the Devil's Gorge, and they put an end to the U-Boat threat to SC 118. This convoy had proved that a combination of strong air and sea cover could fight an even battle with the wolf packs. Twelve merchantmen had been sunk in the five days of battle, but three U-Boats had also been sunk, and four others had been severely damaged. Von Forstner went home to get the Knight's Cross of the Iron Cross for his work. He had already celebrated with his crew on the way home as the award was announced by Doenitz in a message. They had drunk cognac and eaten cake the cook baked for the occasion, feeling lucky to do so. For now, they dared not even break radio silence on the way home and slunk across the Bay of Biscay, which was under constant allied aerial surveillance. *U-402* arrived home a week late, her conning tower marked with the figures 103,000 to represent her total tonnage. But where earlier a captain had to sink 200,000 tons to win the coveted Knight's Cross, times had indeed changed, and few commanders lived so long as to do that much.

A tale of *U-230* gives some indication of the change in Germany's undersea war. *U-230* was a new boat, commissioned in the fall of 1942, and she had radar. According to the new Doenitz order of that winter, she also was equipped with additional anti-aircraft guns on a new platform on the conning tower. And she had Metox, the willing gift of the French collaborators. She sailed from Kiel in January on patrol, stopped in Bergen for minor repairs, and then moved up around the Shetlands. But where once winter weather had been enough to protect the U-Boats, this time she was attacked on the second day of patrol, and only her Metox cross warned her in time to dive before the airplane was on her, dropping depth bombs. She surfaced again at 0430 the next morning but was forced to dive five times in the next few hours, and each she was bombed. Finally she reached the Atlantic, and she was one of the U-Boats that joined in the wolf pack that attacked SC 118. She fought storm and the escorts, rising up, falling into the sea, pitching, tossing, the water running down the conning tower and the inside of the boat sweating. *Leutnant* Siegmann claimed three ships sunk for the U-Boat in that chase; then there were dreary days until they found another convoy early in March and got into it and sank one ship, while the 18 other submarines in the wolf pack also worked. But now, it was harder shooting—the submarine must surface, or come to periscope depth, fire, and then be prepared for the onslaught of the escorts. Every time *U-230* attacked, she was attacked in turn. The good old days were long gone. The sinkings were heavy, but so were the losses in boats. One attack on *U-230* on this patrol indicates the new difficulties.

It was March 10, around seven o'clock in the morning, and *U-230* emerged from the mist and clouds to find the convoy she was trailing. She saw six ships standing in the sunshine, apparently hardly moving. She got ready for action—but just then another submarine torpedoed one ship. The escorts suddenly appeared from behind a freighter—two destroyers—and charged down

on *U-230,* giving her barely time to clear the
bridge and crash dive.

The aftermath of the storm was a swelling sea,
and now in the moment of emergency the big
swells held the submarine locked with surface
tension. She would not dive. The lock was broken
by sending all available hands into the forward
torpedo room to weight down the bow, and then
with agonizing slowness—the sound of destroyer
propellers was growing ever closer—the U-Boat
dived. As she moved downward, a series of eight
depth charges exploded above her, acting as a
huge hammer, pounding her downward, and steep-
ening the angle at which she submerged. Then
around 600 feet, the captain levelled off, and
using one electric motor, began to move in a slow
evasive curve.

Evasion was difficult with more than one escort above: soon the ping-ping-ping of the Asdic
sensors bounced off the hull, and by the sound of
them the crewmen could tell whether the enemy
was coming or going.

Fifteen minutes went by, and the enemy came—
with a rush. A series of depth charges were sent
down toward the hull, and the crewmen counted.
Sixteen of them, all exploding close enough to
rattle a man's teeth, some so near the conning
tower they thought it would be blown off. The
hull groaned audibly. Wood splintered and glass
broke.

Then silence, growing noise, and another rush
by. The sound of the propellers always seemed to
be receding—when with a crash would come the
first of the depth charges. This time there were
24 of them, exploding just where the submarine
had been a moment before when the captain had
turned to evade. More silence, and then a third
rush of noise and more depth charges, so close to

one side that the men were thrown off their feet as the submarine winced under the pressure.

From aft came the dreaded report: propeller packings leaking. The water was coming into the boat aft and dropping the stern, and it was impossible to keep the submarine on an even keel. The chief of the boat worked constantly to adjust the trim but could not get ahead. Nor could the repairs be made successfully while the boat was under attack—the bouncing and the buffeting made it impossible to do much of anything except take the punishment.

And take it they did. For the next *nine hours* the escorts kept after them. Above, the destroyers obviously knew they were still down there, and they would not give up the attack. So every 20 minutes a new rush, a new barrage of ash cans, more leaks, more tension threatened the boat. The water dripped from the inside of the pressure hull and ran down in rivulets to the bilges. The men could not use the heads, and so the bilges began to stink of humanity. With her stern tilted, even with the motors working, the boat sank slowly, foot by foot, until she reached her danger point of 750 feet. Then the worry was increased, because just a little more pressure, even a well-placed depth charge, would crush the pressure hull and send *U-230* tumbling to the bottom, a wasted mass.

But at the end of the day, the escorts tired of their failure or lost contact and perhaps even lost all their charges in the effort to sink the U-Boat. They moved away, and the captain dared to bring the boat up several hundred feet, although he kept her safely underwater, fearing a trap, for another two hours. Then, when the sea was as silent as it ever is, *U-230* surfaced. The foul air came rushing out of the hatch and every man

who could come above decks moved upward and
filled his lungs with huge gasps.

Now came the cleanup. The bilges were cleared,
a filthy job, and the fresh air was fanned through
the boat until she no longer stank below. The
batteries were charged by running the diesels,
and when the charge was high enough the radio
operators informed Berlin of the night and day
action.

On March 16, this boat was part of the 40
U-Boat pack that attacked convoy SC 122, a huge
body of some 60 ships. *U-230* attacked and fired
all its torpedoes, then ducked, because the escorts were after it again. That night she emerged
from the sea and reported that on this patrol she
had sunk seven freighters, displacing 35,000 tons,
and damaged two others, and that she was heading home.

The rest of the pack continued the battle against
convoy SC 122, and then turned to HX 229, and
when the U-Boats had finished (the two convoys
came together and made one great swirling mass
of fighting, with 38 U-Boats attacking and 30
escorts defending), the submarines had sunk 32
ships of 186,000 tons and damaged nine other
ships. This March battle was the greatest sea
battle of the U-Boats during the war, and all of
March represented the high water mark of the
German U-Boats. During the first 10 days the
allies lost 42 ships, and in the second 10 days
they lost 56 ships. The bulk of these ships, by
far, had been travelling in convoys, and it appeared that the U-Boats had evolved a weapon of
attack that made the convoy system obsolete.
And yet, as the Germans achieved their greatest
success, the forces that would defeat the U-Boats
were already in motion. On March 26, a U-Boat
reported on a new convoy heading west. There
was something new to report as the convoy en-

tered the Devil's Gorge of mid-Atlantic: in the area that had always been free for the U-Boats from air attack there would be airplanes; this convoy was accompanied by an aircraft carrier. And sure enough, the carrier's planes managed to prevent a single U-Boat from closing with the convoy.

At the highest level of government—Mr. Winston Churchill's war cabinet—the British had made the decision that the U-Boat menace must be wiped out if the war was to be won. This decision came concurrently with the appearance of the escort carriers, most of them built in the United States, and the closing of the Devil's Gorge, the air power gap of mid-Atlantic. Also, the allies now introduced the Support Group system, which involved the use of four to six anti-submarine vessels which waited at key points and came to action as soon as a report was made of U-Boat attack against a convoy. And from the European air war, long-range bombers were now diverted in force to work against the U-Boats.

The story of *U-230* tells a good deal of what happened to the U-Boats beginning at the end of March, 1943. She came home and on March 25 was in the Bay of Biscay, that area off the Atlantic regarded as a U-Boat lake, because the new submarine base of Lorient was here, and there were also lesser bases in the area. But no longer, the men of *U-230* learned to their chagrin. The U-Boat moved on the surface to use its Metox detection gear, and three times that night had to crash-dive to escape the bombs that fell around her. Next morning the bombing began at 10 o'clock, when a plane swooped down on them. They dived in 18 seconds, and 10 seconds later a series of four bombs blew up so close to the U-Boat that they threw the stern out of the water.

They escaped, but in reconstructing the attack

once calm returned, the captain remembered that they had not had any warning from the Metox. Later that day they learned it was no mistake. They were bombed at noon, and again at 1:30, and again an hour later. The second bombing was so close it damaged the rear diving planes. And in no case was there any warning—either something was wrong with the Metox or the British had a new detection system.

That night the submarine dived three times to escape bombs. Alert to the danger in what had been their lake, they stayed submerged all the next day. Next night they surfaced but had to dive six more times. On the following day they ran submerged at 150 feet and were bombed several times even so. They found safety that night in a fleet of French trawlers, which they accompanied to the area where they were supposed to meet their escort. While they waited they learned that another submarine had been sunk near there while waiting for escort.

Six hours late, the surface escort arrived and took *U-230* into Brest Harbor where she was hidden beneath tons of steel and concrete in one of the U-Boat pens of this new bunker. Then she *was* safe, for the first time since leaving mid-Atlantic. It was a distinct change from the past.

Captain Siegmann went up to make his report to Admiral Doenitz, and the U-Boat men had a party, replete with fine French foods and French wines and girls. They had left Germany after a Christmas so gloomy and ersatz that at their base even the food had been unremarked from any other day except for what they brought from home, but here there was plenty.

U-230 was repaired and refitted for action as the crew went on leave. Then it was April 24, and she sailed on a new patrol, followed out by *U-456*, which was Captain Teichert's boat. After the escort left them, they dived and went their separate ways.

The U-Boat had received an improved radar during the refit, and it helped with detection of the British planes. They reached their target area in the Central Atlantic in May—and now they began to intercept messages of a kind they had never heard before in such volume.

On May 5, they picked up a message from *U-638* to Doenitz. The U-Boat was sinking, attacked by a destroyer. That was her last message. Two hours later came a similar call from *U-531*.

Next day, May 6, *U-438* announced her own destruction by a corvette, and that same day *U-125* called that she was rammed by a destroyer, having first been bombed by a plane, and was going down.

On May 7 came the dismal news that *U-663* was destroyed—and then came plaintive calls from Berlin for *U-192* and *U-531* to report. They were never heard again. A few days later *U-528* was lost.

Something was very much wrong. Doenitz was learning, to his sorrow, of the new allied methods and the new short wave radar, which was so much more effective than the old.

U-230 encountered the new ways on May 12 when she was sent to intercept a convoy as part of a wolf pack. She found the convoy early in the morning but was prevented from attacking by the wall of escort vessels outside it. When the convoy passed, she surfaced to report to Berlin and was almost immediately attacked from the air by a small plane. The U-Boat men could not figure out where the plane had come from. Then it struck them. A carrier.

At mid-day the U-Boat was hunting again—but being hunted also. *U-230* was attacked as she sped along the surface, at 11 o'clock. She was attacked again at 11:42 and dived, then came up 20 minutes later and spotted the convoy ahead. Just then came a report that *U-89* was sinking after an airplane attack, and five minutes later an air attack for themselves.

Suddenly it had become an entirely different kind of war. Now, instead of sending a full complement of the watch to the deck when the U-Boat surfaced, only three men went up, the captain, the executive officer, and one petty officer. They had to be ready to dive at a moment's notice. The decision had been wise—at 1315 they were attacked again by a plane that machine-gunned the bridge and then dropped four bombs so close and so quickly that the U-Boat did not even have a chance to start diving. A few minutes later came a report from *U-456*, Teichert's boat. She had been bombed and could not dive. She was sinking. *U-230* rushed to the scene, saw *U-456* at a strange angle in the water, men on the deck, and yet they could do nothing because a plane was circling the submarine, and a corvette was coming to the scene. *U-230* moved swiftly off, leaving Teichert and his men to their fate.

Just before 1430 that afternoon, another plane came in on them from the stern, but the gun crews of *U-230* fought back this time, damaged the plane, and it went into the sea, blowing up from its own bombs as it hit. A victory—yet an hour later it seemed a small victory as the word came that *U-186* was sinking.

The job of *U-230* was still to attack the convoy, and she proceeded doggedly. At 1600 she was in position, cutting across the front of the convoy. Three minutes later another plane attacked her and this time, even though she dived, the plane dropped a yellow dye marker and when *U-230* surfaced, she found herself in the middle of a yellow puddle in the sea. She came up, Captain Siegmann looked around, and shouted to dive again. This time the attack was coming from a destroyer speeding up to ram.

U-230 clawed desperately for the bottom. Then six depth charges exploded beneath her, threw her out of the water and onto the surface, right next to a British destroyer. The shock was so great that for a moment nothing happened, then the submarine sank again. More depth charges pressed her down, and she hit 700 feet before the chief of the boat could straighten her out.

Again came the depth charging. It seemed worse this day than ever before. It was not just one destroyer, but at least four. And the bombing lasted four hours. Then the destroyer's screws seemed to move away and there was hope. The hope was blasted a few moments later—a whole new group came in to take over as the escorts followed their convoy. By one o'clock in the morning 200 depth charges had been thrown at the *U-230*. Eight hours later the attacks were still occurring regularly, and the boat was in bad shape. Water was rising in the bilges around the feet of the men. The bilge pumps would not work at this depth. The hunter-killer group above continued to shower the boat with explosives.

By midnight the men were wearing breathing masks. By morning of the 14th of May, they were having trouble staying awake in the foul air. They were half suffocated, and the boat was on the edge of its limit of depth tolerance. Still it was 0430 before the attacks stopped and the U-Boat was able to rise to the surface. The men rushed to the open air and after a time took stock. Miraculously the U-Boat had suffered no structural damage and could continue her patrol.

But by now this patrol was telling on the U-Boat men as none had ever done before. They had been without sleep for 70 hours. They made contact with the convoy again, and came under attack again, which precluded rest. Planes found them and bombed them with dye markers. They sped away on the surface to a new area. Another plane attacked and dropped depth charges as *U-230* dived. They picked up a message from *U-657*. The dreadful word: SINKING. Another alarm.

All day long it continued, and yet somehow *U-230* worked her way to the traditional attack position, ahead of the convoy. And then the escorts found them, and it all began over again, down, amid the buffeting, and the crashing of glass and the spinning of instruments. The stink and the wetness and the hard breathing. The tension and the sweating. The smell of chlorine as the batteries got wet.

They stayed down to the absolute maximum of endurance and then surfaced, half expecting to run in under the noses of a destroyer. But they were lucky. There was nothing.

This time, on May 15, when the submarine surfaced, there was damage. A starboard oil tank had broken and had spilled out its oil. That, said the men, thanking the god of the U-Boats, was why the escorts had left them—the destroyers thought they had secured a direct hit and sunk the submarine. But the shortage of fuel was serious. And to add to it was the bending of the starboard drive shaft and the unseating of the starboard diesel engine. The boat was in bad shape. She could not possibly attack again. And so the captain reported his damage to Admiral Doenitz, and reported also that for all his trouble he had not managed to launch a single torpedo against an enemy ship. It was only later that he learned how lucky the *U-230* had been. For six

U-Boats had been sunk in this four-day battle. The men of *U-230* were lucky to be alive.

How lucky they learned as they limped along the surface toward the French coast. Five more U-Boats reported they were under attack—and none came home again. On May 19, *U-954* and *U-273* announced their own deaths, too; attacked by planes, and then silence forever. *U-230* did not have enough fuel to get home, so Doenitz arranged for her to take oil from *U-634* and they fuelled her at sea. On May 23, heading in, *U-230* dived seven times to escape air attack. Next day she was attacked 36 times. On May 25 she was chased by a hunter-killer group of planes. Their depth charging was too much for the shattered electrical system and the boat caught fire in the control room. She *had* to surface and she did. Luck was with her again—the planes had gone away. And it was good that they had; the fire raged below as the men fought it, while the captain conned from the bridge, and the light of the flames rushing up lit up the sky like a beacon, if anyone had been around to see.

The attacks continued as the boat ran for home. There were seven aerial attacks on May 25. The next day the *U-230* was very nearly destroyed when a B-24 came out of nowhere in the darkness of night and bombed them from low altitude, blinding them with a bright light. The captain called the radar operator and chewed him up, but the operator said there had been no impulses on the Metox set. Another attack proved it—there were none. *U-230* had come up against the new big planes equipped with short wave radar and the Leigh lights that enabled them to attack very successfully at night.

May 27, the last day before they reached the continental shelf, was a nightmare; they were attacked nine times, which meant nine crash-dives. They changed tactics, surfacing in daylight so they could at least fight back, and staying underwater at night so the planes could not swoop in on them without notice. And finally, on May 28, quite out of trim, with her after deck submerged and her conning tower bent and damaged, *U-230* limped into harbor at Brest and was safe again. In past the returning U-Boats had been treated as conquering heroes, greeted by bands and flags and ceremony. Now, the men came in silently. No bands were there. They were whisked away to headquarters. The whole atmosphere of the U-Boat war had changed.

CHAPTER EIGHT

The Hunters and Killers

As *U-230* wandered dolefully home in that May of 1943 under heavy attack from allied air and sea power, Admiral Doenitz was making some hard decisions. That month he had lost the fight against the convoys and he knew it. The allied air strength, the increase in escorts, the betterment of depth charges, the new radar all had combined suddenly, and on May 22 he had awakened to the fact that in three weeks he had lost 31 U-Boats. He decided to abandon the wolf-pack technique against the Atlantic convoys until he could make some drastic change that would enhance the fighting power of his submarines.

So on May 24, reluctantly, Admiral Doenitz withdrew the U-Boats from the North Atlantic and moved them into other areas of operations. He had lost the primary battle, which he knew was to sink ships faster than the allies could build them to prevent the amassing of troops and supplies on the English Isles for a future invasion of Fortress Europe.

The U-Boat war must continue, but some changes had to be made while waiting for the strengthening of the U-Boats as weapons, which could come only from the building yards. One change was to put a doctor on each U-Boat to try to cut down the number of casualties and deaths among the crews. A second was to strengthen the U-Boat tactics against allied planes. And in the six weeks that *U-230* was undergoing repairs at Brest, both changes came about. So on July 5, when *U-230* sailed again to go on patrol, she carried with her Dr. Reche, and when she moved out, it was at night, with no cheering section at all, no crowd to betray her departure to the allied agents who seemed these days to know everything. At the tip of the Brittany Peninsula, she was picked up by a Coast Guard ship and then taken to a rendezvous point where she met *U-506* and *U-533*. They would travel together through the Bay of Biscay, using combined firepower to fight off allied air attacks. Doenitz had a new technique, developed by *Korvettenkapitaen* Goetz von Hartmann in *U-441*. Von Hartmann's boat had been armed with two four-barreled AA guns and a semi-automatic quick-firing cannon, and his crew had been trained to a quite different approach to aircraft. Instead of running, they would fight on the surface.

On the days that *U-230* had been struggling for her life to get into the Bay of Biscay and harbor, *U-441* had been out seeking air attack, and on May 24 when a Sunderland flying boat attacked *U-441*, she had slugged it out and shot down the British plane.

In June, *U-758* had gone out for operations using the technique and on June 8 had engaged a British single-engined plane on the surface and drove it off. Two more British planes came in and circled, fired some machine-gun bursts, but stayed well off. Toward evening another plane attacked, coming in low, and was severely mauled by the AA guns. Fifteen minutes later two P-51s attacked, and the U-Boat obviously damaged one of them.

So the technique was getting much approval in Berlin by the time *U-230* was ready to go out.

At the rallying point the three U-Boat captains conferred by megaphone, and *U-553*'s captain explained the procedure. They would travel out at high speed on the surface during the daylight hours. At night they would dive but stay close together and they would surface at dawn. If, while on the surface, a plane was detected, *U-533* would display a yellow flag, indicating that all three boats should crash-dive. If the plane was too close, he would wave a red flag, and all three boats would man their guns and stay together, fighting it out with their concentrated firepower on the surface.

On the morning of July 6 the three boats headed out to sea. Three hours later the yellow flag went up, and like seals, the three submarines dived on schedule. *U-506* had a new device, a radio transmitter that worked underwater, and she gave the order when all was quiet so that the three submarines surfaced simultaneously, in sight of one another, and moved on. So far, so good. Very well in fact.

Early in the afternoon, a B-24 shot out of the clouds and the red flag went up. The three submarines manned their AA guns, and the bombers stayed at a respectful distance. Better and better.

But the B-24 circled the three submarines, and eight or 10 minutes later another B-24 appeared. They both circled. The U-Boat men grew nervous and began firing at the planes.

Five or six minutes later the planes were joined by a big Sunderland flying boat, and a few minutes later another B-24 arrived, making four bombers against three submarines. The four planes attacked, each from a different angle, and forced the submarines to divide their fire power. Men on the guns of the U-Boats began to fall. Four bombs very nearly missed *U-230*, and one gunner was wounded. Towers of water appeared around *U-506*, which dived and then surfaced again. Together the three submarines shot down one plane, the Sunderland, and the three B-24s stood off. The submarines seized the opportunity and all three crash-dived and sped underwater to the accompaniment of detonating bombs. Captain Siegmann started muttering about the idiots at headquarters who figured out the plans that sank submarines. By mutual consent the three U-Boats parted company and ignored the orders that had nearly killed all of them.

It was bad business, no matter how it was done. That week, as *U-230* dodged one air attack after another, remaining alive because she could get down in 18 seconds or less, other boats were going to the bottom to the right and left of her, right there in the Bay of Biscay. *U-514* and *U-232* were sunk on July 8. *U-435* was sunk the next day. Their erstwhile companion *U-506* went down two days later, and *U-409* was sunk that day too. Before they got out of the danger area, they also learned that *U-607* was gone.

U-230's mission was to lay mines off Chesapeake Bay. She was safe enough on the high seas, off the convoy lanes. She was attacked by an American destroyer off the U.S. coast but escaped beneath a layer of heavier water. She laid her mines, 24 of them, and headed home, unhappily serenaded by the wireless transmissions of U-Boats in distress. *U-504*, *U-461*, *U-462* were all bombed and sunk on July 30 in the Bay of Biscay.

U-230 had luck and skill in her crew. She was set upon 400 miles off the American coast by two four-engine bombers and crash-dived. But she seemed unable to shake the pursuers and dived several times each day to escape air attack. Three days later she learned why: Doenitz wirelessed that the U-Boats should all shut off their Metox sets—the allies had gotten onto the transmission system and were homing on the Metox sets themselves. Thus, while the submarine captains thought they were guaranteeing the safety of their boats by using Metox, now they were simply telling the allied planes their location and saying, in effect, "Come and Get Us." Headquaraters later estimated this had been a factor in the sinking of scores of U-Boats.

The officers and crewmen of *U-230* did not know it, but they were a part of the shifting campaign of Admiral Doenitz in this searching time after the failure of the U-Boat war in the North Atlantic, and the mining of the Chesapeake was one of his ploys. That summer of 1943 Doenitz did not hesitate to send his boats out on long missions, secure in the belief that the U-Tanker system was working. He sent several boats to operate in the Indian Ocean. He sent others to work the area west of the Azores, and some to the Gulf of Guinea. These boats operated in the old style, as raider captains had in years past, each with a large area to cover. They began sinking ships. But now the allies were building planes and escorts even faster, and as a boat appeared in an area, the defenses were rapidly strengthened. In July, 30 percent of the U-Boats at sea were lost. Just after the first of August Doenitz cancelled *all* U-Boat sailings until he could get to the bottom of the problem. That is why, on her homeward voyage from America, *U-230* suddenly found herself low on fuel and in deep trouble. She was given a meeting point for refuelling. Then it was changed, without explanation. This happened three times. By August 13, *U-230* was down to two tons of fuel and was floating along to keep at least enough oil for maneuvering. Then came a fourth rendezvous. She was to meet *U-117*, a supply boat, in mid-Atlantic at about the latitude of Cuba. Captain Siegmann estimated the best way to get there and save fuel. He decided to submerge during the day, so he would not have to waste fuel on sudden crash dives, and then to travel very moderately on the surface at night to conserve every gallon of fuel. *U-230* arrived at the rendezvous at the appointed time. The supply boat was nowhere in evidence. She cruised the area. *U-117* simply did not appear. Now *U-230* was in *real* trouble for she had exhausted her fuel. But Doenitz knew, and he had sent two boats to refuel here from *U-117;* as the dispirited men of *U-230* wondered what to do, up came *U-634*, which had almost the same story, with one exception. She still could measure nearly 15 tons of fuel in her tanks. It was not enough to get her home, not enough to help *U-230*, but she could at least move. So *U-634* went to a point many miles away and sent a message to Doenitz in Berlin. The men of *U-230* intercepted and were cheered as much as anyone could be who was sitting, helpless on the surface, waiting.

Doenitz' answer was a shocker. He ordered *U-634* to share her slender supply of fuel with *U-230*, and then both to move to another point to refuel from *U-847* on August 27. It was cutting the margin fine now for two boats instead of just one, but this was a reflection of Doenitz' problem that August, as his tankers were sunk one by one, and he refused to endanger more boats by sending them to sea.

When the day of meeting arrived, five U-Boats were all assembled, four fighting boats and the big *U-847* with her huge fuel tanks. *U-230* got enough fuel for the voyage home and started on a straight line toward the French coast, unable to take any great evasive action or to engage in further operations. Within hours, she learned that U-847, the supply boat, had been sunk. And then came the word that her other rescuer, *U-634*, was hunted down by a corvette. She reported much on August 30, and did not ever report anything more.

U-230 had then to run the gauntlet of allied air power across the Bay of Biscay. Again it was submerge at night and travel cautiously in the daylight. For seven days the U-Boat was harried and depth charged, and almost miraculously she survived to enter Brest Harbor in the second week of September. The chief of the boat came up to the captain as they docked and handed him a cup. Captain Siegmann looked inside. It contained a few drops of oil—all that the boat chief had been able to suck out of the tanks when the voyage was ended.

That same summer, Admiral Doenitz was struggling to secure new weapons for his mauled U-Boat force. New radar receivers solved part of the problem—at least they were not homing beacons for the allied planes. And there was another weapon, the *Zaunkoenig,* the new acoustical torpedo. The new radar made a remarkable effect on the number of sinkings of U-Boats coming through the Bay of Biscay, and Doenitz was considerably gratified. In September, when the first U-Boats to carry the new torpedoes went out, they attacked a convoy on September 20. The battle lasted four days, and it was a reversal of what had been happening. The U-Boat men reported that they sank 12 destroyers and nine merchantmen, while losing two submarines. The British reported the loss of six merchantmen and three escorts, with one escort torpedoed but saved. It was a measure of the permanent change in the battle of the Atlantic that the U-Boat figures could no longer be considered very reliable, and that was because U-Boats had to shoot and then submerge immediately to escape the depth charging that was sure to follow. They could still hear, but the sound of an acoustical torpedo was very much like that of a depth charge. Seldom could a submarine make an unqualified statement that its captain actually *saw* the enemy sink.

Yet Admiral Doenitz' confidence in the *Zaunkoenig,* or wonder torpedo, was not misplaced. This new torpedo could be fired from the most unfavorable position, because it homed on the sound of the propellers of the victim ship. So what happened to that convoy on September 20 is interesting. It was convoy ON 202, and it actually had 41 ships and five escorts. At about the same time the Germans encountered with convoy ON 18, which had 25 ships and nine escorts. So the action was intense.

Late on the afternoon of September 20, *U-641* fired the first acoustical torpedo, which homed right to the destroyer *St. Croix.* She was sorely hurt, and a second torpedo sank her. Three hours later the corvette *Polyanthus* came into the sights of a U-Boat. The acoustical torpedo that hit her caused her to blow up and sink immediately. An hour later *U-666* put a similar torpedo into the corvette *Itchen* and she blew up. The destruction of these three escorts was spectacular; only three men survived from the crews of all three ships.

And yet, the *Zaunkoenig* was a failure. The reason was to be found in the work of American naval Intelligence, whose officers had discovered the secret. Even as Admiral Doenitz sent out his first U-Boats armed with the new weapons, the allies were taking countermeasures.

The secret was discovered when the tanker submarine *U-487* sank after bombing by American planes northwest of Cape Verdes, in July, 1943. Aboard the submarine had been a chief torpedo-mate transferred from the torpedo experiment station at Kiel. He was discovered to have this knowledge and was then persuaded to give naval scientists the information. Soon the allied escorts were towing "foxers," which were noise-makers on the end of a towing line. These attracted the acoustical torpedoes and saved the ships.

By the fall of 1943, the U-Boat men had come to call the Bay of Biscay "Death Valley" because so many of their comrades lay in their iron coffins at the bottom. They had their own magic weapons of defense. One was a balloon filled with helium, strung to aluminum foil. When a radar contact with an enemy was made, a balloon was released on a float, and it was supposed to create a strong image to confuse the enemy radar. But the balloons got tangled up in the superstructure of the submarine, and the aluminum foil stuck to the rails and made the radar blips that much stronger. So the weapon was only partly successful. But by now the Germans had discovered the secrets of British short wave radar and had countered against it, so the submarines had better detection sets.

The real difference was the growing number of surface and air hunter-killer teams that could be put by the allies against the U-Boats. When *U-230* next went out in October, 1943, she had to dive so many times the first night that she was reduced to 70 percent of her battery capacity. Surfacing and submerging, it took her eight days to escape the blockade and patrol zone into mid-ocean. Captain Siegmann had now learned that the secret of survival was to live underwater most of the time, surfacing only when absolutely necessary. It was a theory quite contrary to that with which the U-Boat captains had started the war, but by now it was apparent that only the cautious commanders survived.

U-230 was again out hunting, and in the old way.

She was involved in a wolf-pack attack on a convoy on the nights of October 16 and 17, and the U-Boats sank four allied ships. But six U-Boats were sunk in that two-day battle, and Doenitz called off the wolves. The acoustical torpedo and the new devices were not enough. *U-230* was sent to a different sector of the Atlantic, and Captain Siegmann showed what he was learning. Next time he found a convoy on October 25, he surfaced, quickly assayed the situation, saw the escorts, which were already headed toward him, and gave his executive officer 40 seconds in which to fire torpedoes. The exec did it too, fired four bow torpedoes and one stern shot, and then the U-Boat ran on the surface as fast as she could go to escape three escorts that were after her. Siegmann hit something, but he never knew what. He heard three explosions, but there was no time to see if the ships actually sank. Still, for these times, *U-230* was compiling a very good record: she had sunk four ships and whatever she had to show for this night. It was a far cry from Kretschmer's one-ship-one-torpedo philosophy, but not even a superman could have performed thus in the fall of 1943. The U-Boat force had been cut to pieces. When *U-230* returned to the pens of Brest in November, her crewmen saw that the once-filled bunker was now nearly empty of submarines. The shipyard was quiet. And at the mess the talk was all of friends who had perished in recent months. So many boats were sunk that the Atlantic war was virtually abandoned, north and south. Some boats were sent to the Far East. Others, among them *U-230*, were sent to the Mediterranean to run the dangerous Strait of Gibraltar and base on Toulon.

Back in Berlin, the future was being determined by Admiral Doenitz and his superiors, up to and including the Fuhrer. Doenitz had been hoping for construction of 30 U-Boats a month, and then 40 U-Boats a month. But he knew that even this increase in building would not be enough. The development of new U-Boats and new techniques must be hastened.

The Walter U-Boat was the long-range answer, but it was nowhere near ready for production. A compromise was made, and in the summer of 1943 blueprints were laid out for a 1600-ton boat that could maintain an underwater speed of 18 knots for 90 minutes or travel for 10 hours at 12 knots underwater. This was three times as fast as the Atlantic boats could travel. Admiral Doenitz had now come around to the new philosophy: the U-Boats must be used as submarine weapons. This modified Walter boat could stay underwater for 60 hours. It could be combined with the snorkel and recharge batteries without surfacing. This would be the Type XXI boat. And meanwhile work was also proceeding on a very small U-Boat, also very fast, but displacing only 300 tons, which would be called the Type XXIII. He was hoping that the Type XXI boats would be ready in the spring of 1944 and that large numbers of them would be available by that fall.

These changes were made with some realization of what the allies were doing in anti-submarine warfare. The hunter-killer group, air and sea, or surface only, was certainly one of the most effective of these changes. It depended on location devices, but given those, and the allies were bettering them all the time, one vessel or plane could find the submarine and keep contact with it, all the while informing the "killer" as to the evasive maneuvers the submarine might be taking. An effective new weapon was the "hedge-hog," a launching device which could throw depth charges in groups ahead of the attacking ships to explode on contact. Before, a destroyer rushing down on a submerging U-Boat had to pass over it and wait for the depth charges. Now the de-stroyer could shoot the charges out to hit the submerging U-Boat.

The hunter-killer technique was being bettered all the time. One of the effective changes was the use of escort carriers, and by the beginning of 1944 many of these were available. Typical of this new technique was the Guadalcanal hunter-killer group, under Captain Daniel V. Gallery. He was captain of the escort carrier *Guadalcanal,* and also commander of the group, which included four escort destroyers. These groups truly revolu-tionized the war at sea.

Gallery's group sailed from Norfolk in Janu-ary, 1944, bound for the Atlantic hunting ground. In the way that the U-Boats hunted merchant-men, the hunter-killer group would track down U-Boats. For two weeks the planes flew off from the carrier in the decent weather and returned, with nothing to report. But on January 16, west of the Azores, planes wre launched and started their searches, all around the carrier. They hap-pened upon one of Admiral Doenitz' supply sub-marines fuelling two other U-Boats.

U-544 had come to this position on call and was already pouring oil into the bunkers of *U-129,* through a six-inch hose. *U-516* was also sur-faced, standing not far off, waiting her turn to take on fuel. Suddenly, out of the darkening sky, down swooped two planes and dropped depth charges all around the three. They sank *U-544*, but *U-129* was only damaged, and *U-516* managed to dive in time and get away clean.

The hunter-killer group then had slim pickings for the rest of its cruise. Admiral Doenitz simply was not sending his boats out into the Atlantic. So Captain Gallery went back to Norfolk without more successes to begin a second cruise in March. This time the hunting area was to be between the Azores and Gibraltar. The allies had learned that Doenitz was moving his boats out of the Bay of Biscay and into the Mediterranean, and Gallery was to catch them coming down if possible. The airplanes were now practicing night landings and preparing to work around the clock.

Early in April, several U-Boats sailed from Lorient and Brest. The captains knew that their chances of returning were very slim these ways; this spring nearly 80 percent of the boats sent out were not returning, and the feeling of impending doom overshadowed the messes and the whole submarine force. The commanders of the U-Boats in the early days had been *Korvettenkapitaens* and *Kapitaenleutnants,* men with a good deal of experience and training in the sea and the service. But time had dealt so harshly with Doenitz' force, that now his captains were often *Oberleutnants.* Once such was *Oberleutnant* Herbert A. Werner. He had served in the navy since enlistment at the end of 1939, when he was 19 years old. Fifteen months later he had been graduated from the Naval Academy at Flensburg and assigned to submarines. He had served in *U-557* under Ottokar Paulssen as a *Leutnant.* Submarines carried one or two of these young men, almost as supercargoes, to teach them something. Such were the demands of the service that in November, 1941, Werner was posted to *U-612* as executive officer, which meant torpedo officer and gunnery officer as well. He served, then, as an executive officer until January, 1944, when he was picked to go to commander's school at Neustadt. But in 1944, at 24 years, he found himself a veteran. In his class at commander's school, only he and one other officer had any experience in submarines. All the other young officers had come from destroyers, minesweepers, and the big ships—not one of them had even a single patrol's experience in submarines. Werner finished, as might have been expected, at the top of his class, but his reward was to be given command of one of the old Atlantic boats, *U-415*. When the assignment was handed out, he regarded it as a death sentence.

Now, early in April, he was sailing out into the Atlantic. Doenitz had a new strategy, the old wolf-pack system was gone, but he was using a modification of it—stationing submarines in the areas where the convoys converged. This meant shallow water, 500 feet and less, and no chance for deep diving to escape the hunter-killer groups. Werner was to go to the westerly approach to the English Channel. This also meant the hunter-killer operations would be heavy.

But orders were orders and he sailed on April 11. At about the same time, so did *U-448*, *U-515*, and *U-342* sail from the French ports, to be assigned areas along the convoy route. There were the usual depth chargings and crash-dives to escape the hated planes of the enemy. Werner sighted a convoy and fired four torpedoes in a fan pattern from far outside the perimeter of the convoy. Submarines just did not get in among the ships these days. Immediately, Werner crash-dived; on the way down the crew could hear three explosions, but they did not ever know what they hit. Then for 18 hours they were sub-

jected to relentless harrying by the depth charges
of the enemy. It continued. The hours crept by,
and the men in the U-Boat could tell that the
guard above changed, and new escorts came in to
hunt for them with new supplies of depth charges.
Soon it was 24 hours, then 30 hours, then 36
hours. At two o'clock in the morning of the second day, 39 hours after the torpedoes were fired,
the U-Boat surfaced gingerly when the sounds of
propellers seemed to die away.

U-415 was very lucky. Not so *U-448* and *U-342.*
Doenitz kept calling them, and they did not answer. And as for *U-515,* she had fallen afoul of
Captain Daniel Gallery and the *Guadalcanal*
hunter-killer group. As the U-Boats sought the
convoy lanes, so the hunter-killers sought their
prey in the same place.

On the night of April 5, *Guadalcanal* launched
a flight of four planes, and one of them found and
then lost *U-515. Kapitaenleutnant* Werner Henke
spotted the plane and crash-dived before the pilot could get in to drop his depth charges. But
the pilot reported back to the hunter-killer force,
and an hour and a half later, when Henke had
felt it safe to surface once more to recharge his
batteries, another plane depth charged him and
forced him down. The charges all fell short, but
the hunter-killer group was moving rapidly toward the area now. More planes went out, and
before dawn they again found the U-Boat on the
surface and again missed her. But now the hunter-
killer force was only 15 miles away, and *U-515*
had been so seriously disturbed during hours when
she was supposed to be recharging that she had
done very little of it. And the death hunt was on.

An hour after sunrise, three destroyer escorts
had found the U-Boat by sonar impulses and
were pounding Henke with depth charges. Three
times he escaped, but they continued to search in

a pattern, and the old, slow Atlantic U-Boat could only make about five knots underwater, while the destroyers were more than four times as fast. Four times they found him, the last time at 1300. The depth charging began again. Just a little over an hour later, the damage inside the boat was so great that the *U-515* surfaced, and as she came up, in the middle of four destroyers, all of them opened up on the U-Boat with guns, depth charges, and even torpedoes. Men poured out of the hatch, as quickly as they could come in this hail of fire, and they tried to indicate that they were surrendering. But the hunter-killer group was not having any—not paying any attention to the gestures. So far had the U-Boat war gone that little quarter was given anyone these days.

No U-Boat could withstand the hail of fire. In four minutes *U-515* shot her bow in the air and her stern down and then slid back down into the water, the spume pouring out of her vents as she died. Forty-five men, including the captain, were rescued by the destroyers, but 10 of them did not get out in time and went down with the U-Boat. Two days later, *U-68* was caught in the net of this hunter-killer force, and she was torn in two, leaving only three survivors for the Americans to pick up. By that time, Werner in *U-415* was undergoing his ordeal and would surface to find that Doenitz was calling all the U-Boats home. The word was out that the allies were planning an invasion of Fortress Europe.

One boat that did not make it home was *U-505*, whose captain was *Oberleutnant* Harald Lange. She had sailed from Brest for Freetown on March 16 to work the route of the African and eastern convoys, which were coming around the Cape of Good Hope instead of using the dangerous waters of the Red Sea and the Suez Canal. The pickings were very slim these days, and she had patrolled between Cape Palmas and the Cape of Good Hope, but she saw nothing at which she might shoot except one fast passenger liner that escaped her.

On May 24, *U-505* started home. All went quietly enough until May 29, when her interception gear began to pick up enemy planes, and she dived several times but was not attacked. And yet—the *Guadalcanal* hunter-killer group was on his trail. The reason: Admiral Doenitz' demand on his U-Boats that they keep in constant touch with base so he could keep track of their activity. Allied radio interception had reached such a high degree of proficiency now that *Guadalcanal* was aware of the general area in which *U-505* was located and was beginning to close in on her.

Late in May, *Gaudalcanal* had many transmissions on one frequency and recognized them as those of a U-Boat that was not far off. On the night of June 2, the scouting planes flushed what they were sure was a U-Boat and depth charged the area thoroughly. But next morning there was no indication that they had sunk or even damaged a submarine. The big advantage of a carrier hunter-killer force was that it could cover hundreds of miles, which meant the day's steaming of a submarine, and Captain Gallery stuck around this contact area, trying to find the U-Boat, which was quite within the realm of possibility.

Then on June 4, at 11 o'clock in the morning, the destroyer escort *Chatelain* made a contact. Immediately the chase was on. *Guadalcanal* headed for the area at full speed, in spite of being dangerously low on fuel. Captain Gallery sent two more destroyers to assist *Chatelain,* and so *Pillsbury* and *Jenks* went after the submarine, too.

U-505 was cruising at periscope depth when

the contact came. Suddenly, *Chatelain* was on top of her, throwing depth charges ahead of her, the new hedgehogs, that went out in a salvo of 20. From above, two fighter planes suddenly spotted the shadow of the submarine underwater and dived on her, spitting machine-gun fire and directing the destroyers to the spot at which they were aiming. *U-505* tried to dive deeper. Her batteries were in terrible shape because she had spent so much time underwater in the last few days, when Lange spotted the hunter-killer almost on top of him. He had a real problem. If he dived deep now, he might be depth charged and not get either down or up in time. He hoped to survive the first run and then head for deep water and safety. He kept on, hoping.

U-505 did survive that first attack, but then the planes spotted the submarine for the destroyers and they came in. Another group of depth charges landed virtually on the submarine. It shuddered, the lights flickered and died. The rudder jammed to starboard, and the U-Boat was thrown on her starboard beam, tangling men and crockery and machinery. From the after torpedo room came the shout that water was coming in—which meant the pressured hull had been breached and that the boat would most surely sink in a few minutes.

Captain Lange took but a moment to decide. There was not a chance of saving the boat. All he could do now was perhaps save some of the crew. He ordered the tanks blown and the men to get ready to abandon and scuttle their U-Boat.

As the conning tower broke water and Captain Lange emerged, a 40mm shell from a destroyer burst next to him and wounded him, knocking him out of action. Men picked him up and lugged him off the submarine and into a rubber boat, all the while under fire from the hunter-killer force.

The shooting continued, as the submarine ran around in a tight circle (guided by the jammed rudder). Some of the men made attempts to scuttle, but they were in a hurry to save themselves, and only one large-diameter pipe cover was actually removed to sink her. The men thought she was going to go down anyhow, so 59 of them got out. The only one who did not get saved was one gunner's mate who was killed on deck by the fire from the destroyers.

Men from the *Pillsbury* had been assigned to try to capture the U-Boat, and they rushed down the hatch after the Germans got up. One of the first men heard water gushing up near the periscope well and found an open sea cock. He closed it, and it was lucky for the boarding party that he closed it when he did. The water was so high around the conning tower that swells were beginning to wash down the hatch. Aided by engineers from *Guadalcanal* the boarders managed to find the compressed air valves and keep the boat afloat. They found and disarmed 13 demolition charges, missed one, but the Germans had never set the firing mechanism anyhow.

And so *U-505* was captured, the second U-Boat to be captured during World War II. (The first, *U-570*, was captured by the British much earlier in the war.) The value to the allies was immense; for one thing they captured the German naval codes, and while the navy changed its code several times a year as a precautionary measure, the code books held the key. And for the rest of the war, the allies had the ability to read the Doenitz messages to his U-Boats, for the capture of *U-505* was made a matter of secrecy for this reason.

Still, the codes were not the major factor in the U-Boat war; the growing might of the allied forces and the steady weakening of Germany was the

big factor. By this spring of 1944, it was apparent that the sea war was lost. Indeed, when it
became apparent that the invasion was not far
off, Doenitz' plans for his submarine commanders can be described as nothing less than desperate. One day in May, at the Brest headquarters
of the First Flotilla, the senior officer of U-Boats
West presented the plans for the U-Boats during
the invasion. The commanders of the old Atlantic-
type boats, not equipped with the new snorkels,
were told that they were to attack and sink the
invasion fleet, and *if necessary they were to destroy enemy ships by ramming*. That was desperation! These old boats and their crews were to be
sacrificed.

Then came the invasion, and these boats were
ordered to move on the surface to the English
coast and attack shipping. On the night of June
6—D-Day—the boats began to sail, 15 of them
from Brest. The snorkel boats got through all
right, but the others were caught in a sea battle
between British forces and their own destroyers,
and several of them were sunk. Even the snorkel
boats were going down one by one. The submarine war was entering its last phases.

CHAPTER NINE

Disaster

By the time of the allied invasion of Normandy in June, 1944, Admiral Doenitz could justify the U-Boat campaign only as a means of "tying down" large forces of destroyers, escort carriers, and planes that would otherwise be deployed elsewhere against the Germans. He was depending on the snorkel (or schnorchel) and soon after the invasion he ordered that no U-Boat that did not have snorkel equipment was to go into the Atlantic. Even more, he was waiting with the desperation of a dying man awaiting a medical miracle for the Walter-type U-Boats that were truly "submersibles"—that is boats designed to operate underwater for long periods of time. He had at long last learned the bitter lesson of the radio: that the transmissions were the giveaway. For a time he had tried to get along with a blurt technique—in which the U-Boats transmitted their messages in extremely high-speed flashes, the idea being to get off the air before the HF/DF range finders could zero in on them. But this had not worked either, and by June, 1944, Doenitz accepted the fact that he could no longer control his U-Boat force tactically, but must refrain from use of the radio. "Out of the question," he said of radio, at this time.

U-Boats did achieve success against the allies in the summer of 1944, in and around the invasion areas, but at what cost! They sank five escorts and damaged one, sank 12 merchant ships and damaged five, sank four landing craft and one landing ship. But to do this cost Doenitz 20 of the 30 U-Boats he had put in action for this purpose. Altogether, the sinkings represented about 100,000 tons for those 20 boats. What a difference from the old days, when Otto Kretschmer alone had sunk around 300,000 tons in his one U-Boat.

The ring closed on the U-Boat bases. By midsummer, 1944, the Bay of Biscay became untenable as a base for the German U-Boats, and operations were transferred to Norway that summer and fall. There were many changes then to come in the U-Boat operations.

Brest was a case in point, and the submarine *U-953's* tale shows what was happening. *U-953* was the last U-Boat left in Brest in August, 1944, and very nearly the last boat in France. Toulon, the southern base, had been eliminated when eight U-Boats were bombed and sunk—and that was the end of the U-Boat war in the Mediterranean. By mid-August, the U-Boat flotillas around the Bay of Biscay were being dissolved and the navy men employed as soldiers to defend the land. At Brest naval men were given the task of defending the city bastion. The First U-Boat flotilla and the Ninth U-Boat flotilla were transferred to caves and tunnels, and only a few workmen remained in the navy yard to finish repairs on two boats, *U-247* and *U-953*. *U-247* was finished first and tried to break out through waters controlled by the allies. She was lost with all her crew. Then came *U-953*.

This U-Boat was commanded now by *Oberleutnant* Herbert Werner, whose *U-415* had been sunk in the harbor in Brest by a British mine. *U-953* was declared fit on August 19, although her diesel engines were in poor shape, her batteries were old and tired, and the boat was only half safe. But there was no time. She would not even carry torpedoes—her job was to get the most valuable engineering equipment out of the base and to La Rochelle, where there was still a chance of shipping it overland and back to Germany.

The departure of *U-953* from Brest was unlike any the U-Boat men had experienced before. They had to fight off civilians and others, at gunpoint, because they insisted on being taken aboard the boat. In all, 100 people were taken on August 22, when the U-Boat sailed. Already American tanks were breaking through into the naval compound. The boat had an escort, moved on the surface to the submarine net, and then outside. Immediately the ships were detected by the British, who lay in wait. That day crewmen of *U-953* listening to allied radio had been addressed and warned that *U-953* would never make it out of port. She stopped with the warning that British torpedo boats were awaiting her. Then she saw them, a dozen of the enemy, and she turned and raced back to the safety of the port near dawn.

Early on the morning of August 23, *U-953* tried again, because there was no alternative: sail or be captured. But Captain Werner decided to take her out wihtout an escort and submerged. He dived and made his way through the flotilla of torpedo boats, running on the submarine's electric motors. Depth charges began to detonate, but in the distance. The little boats knew he was out, but they did know where. Three hours after diving, *U-953* managed to get into water deep enough to submerge to 100 feet and headed southwest, bumping the bottom and floating with the prevailing current. She went with the tide, at high tide. Just before 10 o'clock in the morning, when low tide came, Werner stopped the boat on the bottom and sat there as dozens of destroyers and other boats churned above him, searching. In mid-afternoon he headed out to sea and managed to evade his torturers. He had not even dared to use the snorkel yet, for fear it would betray his position.

The snorkel came out of water at three o'clock on the morning of August 24: the U-Boat was brought up to 50 feet, the mast for the snorkel was run out of its telescope, and the valves were opened. Fresh air began to come into the boat. That night the U-Boat moved slowly through the Bay of Biscay, underwater, charging its batteries, stopping frequently to check sounds and to be sure there no pursuers. On August 28, the boat arrived at La Rochelle. Four days later Werner was ordered to take her to Norway. He was lucky—the officers and crews of half a dozen other U-Boats had to abandon their submarines and make their way overland, fighting to get home. Most of the men of *U-123*, *U-129*, *U-178*, and *U-188* did not make it back to Germany. Their boats had been blown up before them.

Again, in La Rochelle, *U-953* was the last boat in the pens that had once housed 40 U-Boats. On September 7, Captain Werner and his crew headed out to sea on patrol, the last U-Boat to leave France. He was given his orders to operate in the shallow waters of the North Channel, between the Irish coast and Scotland.

Hugging the shore, the U-Boat made its way out seaward and dived before dawn, to use the snorkel. On the second day of snorkelling they encountered one of the device's great disadvantages. In a rough sea, the wind swept the seas over the snorkel float, and it closed the valve; the engines continued to suck air, and in effect sucked the air out of the boat creating a semi-vacuum, which tortured the men's ears and took their breath away. But this was safety. There was no other.

As they moved north, the orders changed. Admiral Doenitz instructed Werner and three other boats, all those abroad in the Atlantic, to form a patrol line along the western entrance to the North Channel.

Perhaps. Perhaps because *U-953* was beginning to break down from overuse and bad maintenance of recent weeks. There was fire in the control room. A pump quit suddenly. On September 16 the starboard diesel went out. Broken bushing. The snorkel stuck and had to be loosened. On the one diesel it was difficult to charge batteries. An air intake valve failed and the boat went down nearly to 800 feet and oblivion before she could be stabilized. It took two days to repair the snorkel this time. While they waited, the men heard of the death of two more U-Boats, two of the very few remaining.

The gyro-compass failed, which meant they were without means of navigation. Captain Werner grounded the boat until it was fixed. The port diesel clutch jammed. And now the U-Boat had to lie on the bottom of Sligo Bay while both diesels were repaired. Obviously she was not sinking any enemy ships this way.

U-953 went into the North Channel and saw many escorts and British warships there but did not attack destroyers or corvettes. Werner was saving his torpedoes for merchant ships, knowing Doenitz' desires and not wanting to commit suicide. But on September 29 the snorkel cable broke, with the snorkel in position. They could not lower it, which meant that if they dived deep it would break off. Nor could they make a periscope attack with the snorkel in place. So they had to find a German base and go in for repairs. The patrol was over, having accomplished nothing. They headed for their new base at Bergen in Norway.

U-953 was harried all the way. She escaped through one hunter-killer group of six destroyers, dodged others, and arrived off the Shetland Islands in the second week of October. Forty miles farther and she was beset by a hunter-killer group for 28 hours—unable to dive deep, unable to surface. And finally she arrived in Bornjefiord. *U-953* was in such bad shape that the decison was made to rebuild her in a shipyard in Germany, and Werner and his crew then took her there. Late in October they arrived at the yard in Lubeck-Siems and learned that the rebuilding would take 10 weeks. So in five months this particular U-Boat had accomplished one mission, to move engineering equipment from one lost port to another that would soon be lost. She had sunk no ships at all. It was a measure of Admiral Doenitz' frustration in the autumn and winter of 1944.

For years Doenitz had pleaded for his new weapons. Now they were very nearly ready. Eight of the small Type XXVII boats were almost completed, and in May 63 would be ready to fight. As for the Type XXI U-Boats, they were even more effective weapons than Doenitz had hoped. But they would not be ready until May. When they were ready, let the allies look out!

But at the moment, in December, 1944, Doenitz' U-Boat war still had to rely on Atlantic U-Boats fitted with snorkels. Even the new boats of this type were to have their troubles as did Captain Heinz Schaeffer of *U-977* which was commissioned just before Christmas, 1944. It would be April before she would be ready to go to sea, and before that Schaeffer had to evacuate the base at Pillau in East Prussia and move west to Wesermuende.

Schaeffer seemed no better off than Werner in his old boat. In fact, Werner's was ready sooner, in February. He was not happy with the state of the boat. He discovered that the executive officer and his chief of boat were both inexperienced, but he could do nothing about it. His junior officer, an ensign, was a politician, a Nazi, and kept the boat stirred up with his talk. Werner did not like that but couldn't do anything about it, either.

Captain Werner had a glimpse of the state of the war just before he sailed on his February patrol. He was called to Doenitz' headquarters outside Berlin, and there, with five other U-Boat captains, he was given a pep talk by the admiral. Doenitz spoke of their mission: to tie down the allies in the waters around Great Britain and to keep up the U-Boat fight until the new superboats would be ready. Although all five of the other officers were newcomers to the service, captains without U-Boat experience, Doenitz promised them all a new superboat when they came back from this patrol in the old boats. And as for the importance of what they were doing, Doenitz said he could not overemphasize it. He was ready to send every conventional U-Boat out. Werner came away in a state of shock with the feeling that defeat was inevitable.

And so in February, 1945, *U-953* sailed. On her first dive, a loading hatch cracked, and the boat began to ship water. It was out of the question that she should run by snorkel for seven or eight weeks, as Werner had anticipated. She could not stay under at all. She surfaced, there in the Skagerrak, and immediately was attacked by British planes. Her radar went out, and she was very close to defenseless. She sailed to one port, and then another, and finally had to make Bergen—

all this on the surface creeping along the coast at night—and made Bergen. Captain Werner considered it next to a miracle. There, he had the hatch welded shut; it was the only way to make a quick repair. The radar was repaired. He sailed again.

As *U-953* moved toward his patrol position, he learned that half a dozen U-Boats had been sunk in the past few days. That meant his friends from the meeting with Doenitz, all on their first patrols. British defenses had increased tenfold since the old days.

U-953 was assigned to operate in Plymouth Bay, and there she went, in spite of the obvious danger. For weeks she travelled submerged, using the snorkel. She was attacked on March 19, by destroyers that came on her by accident. Apparently they did not believe their own radar, for the attack was halfhearted and quickly ended without damage. Next day she saw a convoy of seven ships with four escorts. At last here was an opportunity for Werner to avenge all that had gone before. He ordered the tube doors opened and ready for firing. It was a chance like none he had enjoyed for months.

The doors jammed.

Worse, they froze half open, which meant they could not withstand a depth charging. No hope for repair here at sea. They had to go back to Norway! It was now April 7, 1945. Another patrol had ended without a single victory. Almost immediately the boat was moved to Trondheim, and there Captain Werner discovered that *U-953* would be months under repair. There was much talk about the use of 60 old boats and the coming new boats, and how Britain would soon be surrounded by 150 U-Boats which would cut off the supplies to the continent. But as for Werner, he was to go to Oslo and wait for another U-Boat, at Horten, or at Kristiansand.

As April came, Captain Schaeffer of *U-977* found himself considerably upset. Here he had a new boat, but its batteries were only 70 percent effective, and there were many other defective parts of the submarine. Further, many of his enlisted men were completely inexperienced. He complained and got nowhere. There was nothing to be done, said the superior powers. He was ordered to Kiel to take on supplies and sail on patrol.

At Kiel, Captain Schaeffer requested a personal interview with Admiral Doenitz. A submarine captain could still get that privilege, even though Doenitz was now chief of the whole navy and a very exalted figure. But that was all. When Schaeffer complained about the condition of the boat and the training of the crew, Doenitz offered him small sympathy. That was the way it was, he said, and there was nothing to be done. If Schaeffer could not take a boat to sea, then no one could. And, said the admiral, hardening, there was no question about it: Schaeffer must take *U-977* to sea as she was.

The captain returned to his command and made ready for sea. In trials in Kiel Harbor, accompanied by another boat readying for sea, *U-977* was bombed by planes, and the other U-Boat was sunk right behind her. But *U-977* escaped. A few days later, she sailed for Norway, along with one of the boats of the new XXI class, the first to be put in service.

Here was Admiral Doenitz' dream come true at last. The Type XXI was equipped with an anti-radar snorkel head, which had its own radar search receivers. So the planes coming over could be located from a long way off. She had an ultrasensitive hydrophone system with a range of 50 miles. She could locate ships while submerged, avoiding escorts and finding convoys or merchantmen. She had a supersonic echo device which gave course, range, speed, and number of targets. She carried a new acoustic torpedo that would not be fooled by "foxers." Her torpedoes could be fired from any angle. Her underwater power derived from a huge battery, and her propellers were noiseless at five knots. She could sail underneath a convoy and launch torpedoes from 150 feet and attack without ever seeing the enemy or being seen.

The allies had nothing to match her and nothing to counteract her. If 20 or 30 of those Type XXI U-Boats got to sea and began operating, they could, indeed, play havoc with the allied sea lanes. She had six tubes instead of four forward, and special storage for 14 extra torpedoes. She was the most dangerous weapon to be completed during the war.

The first of the Type XXI's was given to *Korvettenkapitaen* Schnee, and it sailed from Bergen on operations on April 30. Schnee could tell from the beginning that his would be a different kind of war. In the North Sea he picked up a sound contact with an anti-submarine hunter-killer group. He did not have to run deep and lie doggo. Not at all. He altered course by 30 degrees and speeded up, underwater, to 16 knots. *U-2511* then shot away from the anti-submarine group with the greatest of ease. At the end of one hour, her ability to speed was nearly exhausted, but she was far away from her enemies.

Meanwhile, several of the Type XXIII boats were at sea. *U-2321* remained at sea for 33 days, even though this was a small boat, carrying only a few torpedoes. *U-2336* went into the Firth of Forth and sank two ships. She was so small that while the British knew she was somewhere about, they could not locate her with radar.

CHAPTER TEN

Defeat

On May 2, while Captain Schnee was moving gleefully in search of targets, certain that he was in command of a superweapon, and while Shaeffer in *U-977* was beginning a patrol to Southampton Water, Captain Werner, late of *U-953*, arrived in Oslo and then in Kristiansand. He was informed that his new boat had not yet arrived and he went down to the harbor. There he saw two old U-Boats and one of the new Type XXIII boats. He also saw an old friend, who was in command of it, and heard that the boat had just crossed the Skagerrak under constant fire from enemy planes. Berlin had fallen. The U-Boats had left Kiel under direct fire from the enemy *on land* there, from cannon on Tirpitz Pier itself. All the U-Boats that could move had tried to escape. At least seven of them had been destroyed.

A few hours later, it was all over for *Oberleutnant* Werner as a U-Boat commander. The word came from Doenitz to stop shooting against allied shipping. For five years the U-Boat men had fought on the seven seas, but now they were to lay down their arms.

At sea in *U-2511 Korvettenkapitaen* Schnee accepted the inevitable and turned back from his

175

patrol toward Bergen. But he could not resist a
last gesture as a fighting man, even though it
would be known to the enemy only as told: he
made contact with a British cruiser and a handful of destroyers, approached within 500 yards
and made a dummy attack. He was completely
unnoticed by the British; if he had fired his torpedoes undoubtedly he would have sunk the enemy. The weapon was just as fearsome as Doenitz
had hoped. But Schnee came back to port with
U-2511. She was now a part of the spoils of the
victors. The U-Boats at sea were ordered to port.
The captain of *U-1023* surfaced that day, reported that he had sunk an 8000-ton ship and a
destroyer and damaged a 10,000-ton ship. Then
he noted that he was heading for port to surrender. That was the order to the boats at sea: head
for an enemy port and give up.

As for the boats near land, and the U-Boat
men ashore, it was a harder story. Even after the
capitulation, allied planes and ships were leery
of U-Boats, and several of them were sunk around
Norway, bringing the total of U-Boats sunk to
nearly 800. The U-Boat men were kept in Norway or moved for questioning. Eventually many
of them were sent to concentration camps. Werner, no longer an officer but a prisoner, was held
by the British for a time and sent to Frankfurt.
Then he was aboard a train turned over to the
French, who proposed to make laborers of them.
He escaped and was recaptured and sent into
France in a cattlecar with other prisoners. He
was pressed into joining the French Foreign Le-
gion and held in a camp near Cormeiller en
Parisis. He was there until the end of October
and then escaped again and made his way by
train back to Frankfurt, where he hid for a time,
and then gradually integrated himself into civil-
ian life.

As for the boats still at sea, like Captain Schnee's, each commander had to make his own decision, each of the 43 captains. Twenty-three of them headed for Britain, and three went to the United States, while four went to Canada. Seven others made the Norwegian ports or Kiel. One boat ran aground, and another struck a mine, and two others were beached off the Portuguese coast.

Captain Heinz Schaeffer had the same problem of decision as all the others. There had been talk within the U-Boat force of what might occur when defeat came, for very few of the U-Boat commanders could believe at the last that there was any posssibility of victory, wonder weapons or no wonder weapons. One plan under preparation by some in the U-Boat force was *Regenbogen* or Rainbow. When that code name was flashed, had the plan succeeded, all the U-Boat captains would scuttle their boats.

And there was another line of thinking. Several U-Boat commanders gave serious consideration to trying to continue the war as individuals. They did not go very deeply into problems of supply and repairs of course. These romantics were guided by despair and habit and resentment as the last days came. One such was *Oberleutnant* Werner of *U-953,* who made serious plans to escape to Argentina or Uruguay. Just before the end he secured the necessary charts and figured courses and fuel consumption. He mentally sorted out his men, planning to take only unmarried men, and a skeleton crew at that. Even after the surrender, Werner and others were talking of taking U-Boats and escaping. But he did not.

Other captains did, in fact, follow the Rainbow plan and did scuttle their U-Boats. More than 200 boats were thus lost to the victors (who ended up scuttling some themselves). And as for the men in this service, they proved to be the most expendable of all German military people. More than 39,000 of them served in the U-Boats, during the war, and at the end of it only 7000 survived, among them a handful of captains and men who had been in at the start of it. Next to espionage it was the most dangerous service of all.

Even after the surrender, however, there was still one drama to be played out in the tale of the U-Boats. Two U-Boat commanders refused to scuttle or to surrender and made their ways to South America. One of these was Captain Schaeffer in *U-977*.

Schaeffer had been given one pep talk by Doenitz himself just a few weeks before. When he got to Norway in April, he heard the Doenitz broadcast stating that the U-Boat force would never give up. And when he sailed on his last patrol from Kristiansand, the flotilla commander had exhorted captain and crew to fight on to the end, because Germany would never surrender.

On this last patrol, *U-977*'s snorkel let them spend most of their time underwater, but they had the Doenitz broadcast telling them of the end of the war. They also received other broadcasts, from German and allied sources, including one from the allies calling on them to surface and fly a black flag. But Schaeffer simply did not believe the broadcasts, they were so completely at variance with his instructions from Doenitz and his last instructions from his flotilla commander. So he decided to ignore them and follow his own course.

Several days after the German surrender, he called the crew together in the boat and spoke with great feeling. He told them that Germany had lost the war, and he suggested to them that the allies would now make of Germany a vast wasteland and that all German men would be sterilized while German women would become the playthings of the victorious enemies.

He outlined the courses: surrender, or scuttle, or head for Argentina. The U-Boat had the stores, he said, and they could make it. He put it up to the crew.

The crewmen of *U-977* debated, and finally they voted. Thirty of them opted for South America. Two wanted to go to Spain, on the theory that they could wait out the painful postwar period there and then return home when peace was truly established, and the parade of the victors had ended. Sixteen men wanted to go home.

Captain Schaeffer could not have 16 discontented men in U-Boat and that he knew, so he decided to put them ashore in Norway. On May 10 they moved in along the Norwegian coast, avoiding the bright lights of cities and towns, and went in so close to shore to land the 16 men that they ran aground, in the darkness.

The 16 homeward-bound men were moved off the boat into a pair of rubber dinghies and after capsizing one, they squared away and began rowing quietly in toward the shore. The boat was lightened by more than a ton then, but she was stuck on a rock, with her bow pointing up in the air at an angle of 30 degrees. And dawn was about to break.

They tried one thing and another and finally to blow her off with compressed air by dropping the keel with full ballast tanks, then blowing them suddenly, creating a current that would help the propellers. And that was how they got *U-977* off the rock.

Soon they were moving southward, on the course they set for their escape. As light came on in the day, lookouts at the coastal batteries spotted the

U-Boat and opened fire on it. She was at large six days after the surrender, and that was much too long.

But *U-977* escaped and headed around the British Isles, then to move southward through the Atlantic. By day she moved slowly along at 180 feet, making five knots. At night she moved up to within 50 feet of the surface, so the snorkel could send fresh air into the boat. For 18 days the *U-977* remained underwater. The garbage piled up in the boat because there was no way to dispose of it underwater, and it rotted and the worms bred in it.

Meanwhile, *U-530* was doing the same, for she, too, had been stationed at Kristiansand, and her captain, *Oberleutnant* Otto Wermuth, was also sure he must not surrender. *U-530* had gone out a little earlier than *U-977,* and Wermuth at war's end found himself off the coast of Long Island. But rather than surrender, he headed for the River Plate, too.

The boats had their troubles, with diesels and snorkels and the tension of living underwater for days on end. After seven weeks the tempers of the men of *U-977* were ready to explode, and they quarrelled over such matters as whether or not they should unload their torpedoes. Schaeffer argued that they must keep them intact, as evidence of their good faith and the fact that they had carried out no attacks since the surrender. Wermuth's boat was more suspect, for in those last hours he had expended all his torpedoes at ships off the American coast.

There was one emergency after another aboard *U-977*. The men developed boils and rashes from salt water they used to wash their clothes and the constant dampness and mold of the boat. One man injured his hand and then his whole arm became infected and Schaeffer had to operate.

Some men objected to the long voyage and wanted to go into a Spanish port, but Schaeffer overruled them.

The two boats moved on their separate courses, almost always underwater. It was only after 60 days that Schaeffer felt they must surface *U-977,* and he resisted for another six days, to emerge from the sea in the Atlantic off Gibraltar. He still had a long way to go.

In a way, Schaeffer and *U-977* were lucky. For Wermuth and *U-530* arrived in Argentine waters in July, just about two months after VE-Day. They sailed into the River Plate and hoped to be treated as friends. But Argentina had entered the war in the last days on the side of the allies, and now the Americans wanted *U-530,* particularly when they learned Wermuth's story and how he had come from the American station where he had been fighting at the last moment. The absence of his torpedoes was not very helpful, either.

U-530 was interned and so were the crew. Then they were given over to the Americans as prisoners of war. This word was broadcast by the Argentine radio and picked up by the worried men of *U-977* who were still far out in the Atlantic.

Schaeffer was ready for a fight at any time. The U-Boat surfaced at night and dived in the daytime and kept its anti-aircraft guns in good repair. Had he encountered an ambitious allied escort vessel or plane there would have been one more little footnote to the battles of World War II, but luckily for *U-977* their course did not cross that of any enemy.

The U-Boat was short of fuel. She had used half her 80 tons in the first difficult rush through the North Sea and then down the North Atlantic. But by careful husbandry, by diving only when necessary and using the diesels at slow speed and the electric motors more than half the time, they could just make it, Schaeffer figured.

On they went, and as the tensions grew, one of the officers seemed intent on bringing about a mutiny. Schaeffer relieved him and humbled him before the crew. They stopped at the Cape Verde Islands briefly, and morale rose. The men began to come up and take sunbaths, and as their health improved, morale rose higher. They camouflaged their boat, and even rigged a fake funnel, so they would look like a surface vessel if chanced upon by ship or plane.

They considered scuttling the boat off Brazil and trying to escape in little groups, but Schaeffer told them their chances were very slim and they stuck with the submarine. Finally, on August 17, 1945, *U-977* reached Argentine waters and surrendered the boat to officers of the Argentine navy. Schaeffer had hoped to start a new life in Argentina, but he found himself a prisoner. Furthermore, he found himself under deep suspicion on two counts. The Brazilian ship *Bahia* had been sunk somehow after the surrender. The charge was made that she was the victim of a renegade U-Boat, and the allies suspected that *U-977* was the renegade. Schaeffer showed them his 10 torpedoes, but since a U-Boat could carry 14 torpedoes, that did not convince the investigators. He showed them his log, and his readings indicated that the *U-977* was far away from the point of sinking on the day that *Bahia* went down.

There was, then, another suspicion—after the end of the European War: as to the fate of Adolf Hitler and Martin Bormann and other high Nazi leaders. The rumor was out that Hitler had not died in the Berlin bunker at all but that he had escaped by submarine to Argentina where there was known to be a strong Nazi colony. Argentine

newspapers and particularly Uruguayan newspapers speculated on the charge that Captain
Schaeffer was an international agent and that he
had brought Hitler to South America. The charge
was taken very seriously indeed by allied investigators, and Schaeffer was taken to Washington
for interrogation. It was many months before the
Americans were convinced that he had not spir-
ited Hitler and other Nazis away at the end.
Then the crew and finally Captain Schaeffer were
sent back to Europe, but there the British recaptured Schaeffer and began again to interrogate
him about his supposed rescue of Adolf Hitler.
Finally it ended, and eventually Schaeffer was
freed and made his way to Argentina to live. He
was one of the last of the captains.

The story of the U-Boats must end with Admiral Doenitz and his remarkable career. His whole
life had been the navy, and more particularly the
submarine arm. He had served in U-Boats in
World War I, his *UB-68* was lost in an accident
at sea, and he was captured and held in a British
prisoner of war camp until the summer of 1919.

Doenitz' career was such that he was asked if
he would like to remain in the naval service. He
replied that if the naval high command expected
to have U-Boats again he would stay in. The
answer was yes, and so he stayed. In all the
years thereafter, Doenitz served in surface vessels, until 1935, when he was chosen to head the
new U-Boat arm of the German navy. All these
years his heart had been with the U-Boats, but
there were none. Under the terms of the peace
treaty, Germany's naval force was extremely lim-
ited and U-Boats were forbidden. But there was
no law that could cover study and development
of tactics, and Doenitz became known as the master of new submarine tactics. It was his idea that
a submarine should attack on the surface and in

the night. It was his idea that the submarines should be used in wolf packs. He fitted himself into the German naval machine, and then in 1935 the British agreed that the Germans could build U-Boats again, and Doenitz' life changed. He was able to develop the Type VII Atlantic U-Boat, which was the most effective weapon the Germans had at sea in the early days of World War II.

Before the war ended, Doenitz had given approval to the development of Plan *Regenbogen,* the scuttling of the German fleet to keep it out of the hands of the enemy. But at the end, he was chosen as Hitler's heir, chief of state, and became responsible for the conduct of Germany. He countered his order to scuttle, and on the night of May 5 went to bed. That night a group of U-Boat men descended on headquarters and bearded the chief of staff. They argued, and then left, with the clear implication that they ought to disregard the admiral's counterorder. And so Plan Rainbow did go into effect and more than 200 boats were sent to the bottom of the sea by their own crews. The allies had the Type VII and all the other boats, and they were not very much aroused, except by the scuttling of two experimental Walter boats at Cuxhaven. That did disturb them, for there was much to be learned from those boats.

Doenitz was in a peculiar position. As head of the U-Boat war, head of the German navy, and finally head of the German state, he was bound to be brought to trial by the allies who had set upon the idea of holding war crimes trials to see who was responsible for the German war movement. From the beginning there was no doubt about the outcome of the trials: the victors would punish the vanquished. Doenitz wanted to defend the navy and the U-Boat service, however,

and that was his defense: that as a naval officer
he used a certain weapon in its most effective
way. The weight of the charge was that as commander of the U-Boat force, Doenitz had caused
the slaughter of survivors of torpedoed ships. The
famous *Laconia* order was brought out to be used
against him.

The trials continued through the summer of
1946, and then, as everyone expected, Doenitz
was convicted of preparing war of aggression and
violating the laws and customs of war by his
conduct of the U-Boat war. Yet while the political
defendants such as Hermann Goering and Rudolf
Hess were given death and life sentences, and
Admiral Raeder was sentenced to life, Admiral
Doenitz was given only 10 years of imprisonment.

One reason for the lightness of the sentence
was probably the testimony produced by a ques-
tionnaire the defense submitted to Fleet Admiral
Chester Nimitz of the United States navy about
the American war in the Pacific. That war, said
Nimitz, had been conducted as a total war against
Japan. Submarines had been ordered to attack
without warning all merchant ships they saw.
American submarines did not rescue enemy survivors if it meant additional risk or interference
with the submarine's operation. In fact, they prac-
tically never considered rescuing the Japanese
enemies.

The British, too, had accepted the U-Boat war
as total war. They told their merchant ships to
report all submarines. They ordered them to ram
U-Boats if possible. They ordered the naval forces
to sink without warning ships encountered in
the Skagerrak, which were almost certain to be
German.

So it became apparent in the Nuremberg trials
that the U-Boat war, as frightful as it was, represented the kind of war that had to be fought

with these particular weapons. And then, at the end, it was apparent that the next war would be even more dreadful and that the U-Boats would play a more frightening role. The Type XXI and the Walter boat were only the beginning. The U-Boats' grandchildren, the missile-carrying atomic submarines, were to become even more frightening.